Submissive Women

Erika Sanders

Submissive Women

Erika Sanders

Series

Submissive Women

Synopsis

It consists of the following novels:
    Submissive
    Fantastic Girl
    The Undressing Game
    Submissive Latin Woman

Submissive Women is a series of novels with a strong BDSM erotic content and, in turn, belonging to the **Erotic Domination and Submission** collection, a series of novels with a high romantic and erotic BDSM content.

(All characters are 18 years or older)

Note about the author

Erika Sanders is an internationally known writer, translated into more than twenty languages, who signs her most erotic writings, far from her usual prose, with her maiden name.

Index

SUBMISSIVE WOMEN
ERIKA SANDERS

SUBMISSIVE

13

I want you.

Everything about you.

From head to toe and everything in between.

Your body, your mind, your soul.

The blemishes you hate that I don't.

I love every part of you, just the way you are.

Especially that ass.

I want to be with you.

All the time.

It doesn't matter where you are.

My mind wanders, triggered by a thought or an image.

A song.

Your initials on a license plate.

A simple word spoken in passing that has a special meaning for both of you.

A stranger who wears hair like you.

Dress like you.

I want to hear your voice.

When you call me with your pet names.

Tell me that you love me, you miss me.

Describe how your day was.

Ask me about mine and give me your opinion.

Share what we are doing or planning.

Even the mundane.

Seduce me late at night as I lie naked in bed in the dark and you are miles away.

Be hard on me when I get spoiled and pout to hang up the phone to sleep or to get you ready for work.

I want to see your interior open in writing.

I savor every new message and photo.

I review past conversations.

I remember that when we are not physically together, you still think of me.

That can be there with a touch of your fingers.

Your words are strong even though there is no sound; They touch me in the background, as if you had said them directly in my ear.

I want to discuss my novels with you.

Please give me ideas as we brainstorm the plot and character names.

Eliminate problem areas.

Get dizzy with the comments and opinions of the fans.

Appease my anger and confusion when faceless and heartless readers criticize my stories for no good reason.

And I continue to write another day with your encouragement.

I want to be tamed by you.

To cook and do housework.

Do errands.

Go dancing, see a movie, and go on trips.

Just snuggle up and take a nap on the couch on a rainy weekend.

Calling me eager to make love under stacks of blankets in bed all day.

Sleeping in each other's arms at night and then waking up next to each other in the morning.

Shower together.

Have make-up sex when we fight.

I want to be kissed by you.

Repeatedly.

Both tenderly and abruptly.

You know how to make fun of me.

Satisfy me.

Wake me up with your lips, teeth and tongue.

To make me cry and moan.

Supplicate.

My body trembles.

I want to do kinky things with you.

Attend meals and events.

Make friends in your lifestyle.

Participate in sexual games at parties.

Discover more secret wishes.

Release our inhibitions.

Explore our darker sides.

Taking each other to the top of the highs and then comforting each other when we dip to the lowest of the lows.

I want to be dominated by you.

He growled because I'm yours.

You make my pulse race and my breathing stop when I hear your orders.

Silent or abrupt, both situations make me blush.

I really want you to pin me against the wall with your cock between my legs, pressed against my pussy.

That you order me to fuck you ... to come only when you say so.

I have no choice but to give in when you torture my ears, neck, and breasts with your mouth.

Or when I feel your hands on my body while you claim yours.

My chest swells with pride when you say that I am a "good girl" for doing what you want.

I want to be tied up by you.

Physically.

Mentally.

With your hands, handcuffs or ropes.

My wrists held in your grip above my head or secured to the head of the bed.

Restricted legs, together or apart.

My movements and reflexes controlled.

Any chance of touching you eliminated.

A blindfold over my eyes so I can't see what you're going to do to me.

I want to be fucked by you.

Naked and overwhelmed under your body as you sweep me away.

Standing free from restraints without a touch from either of you, using just your words to make me squirm and moan while you ruin my mind deliciously.

Or the simple, light touches that you've found bring out multiple orgasms no matter where you stroke my body.

I want you to use me.

Being dragged from one place to another at will.

Overwhelmed when I fight.

My bare ass pounded while you held me.

My toys used on me ... by you.

Your hand gripping my hair on the back of my neck.

Pressing lightly on my throat as you look into my eyes.

To remind me who is in charge.

I want to obey your rules.

When you're out of my reach, they give me something to focus on.

They are defined with my best interest in mind.

I know you will be disciplined accordingly if I break them.

That you trust me to be honest with you when I have disobeyed you.

I want you to comfort me.

Cuddled up against you when I'm overwhelmed or having a bad day.

My hair caressed and kissed with my head nestled under your chin against your chest.

Calmed by your words and your arms around me.

Rocked until any tears stop.

I want to take care of you.

To hug you when you are sad, tired or sick.

I will be your strength, someone to lean on, because even a Dom can have weak moments.

As your sub, I am here for you in any situation that you need me.

To please you or ease your pain.

I want all these things and more.

Because I'm submissive that way.

As you dominant ...

FANTASTIC GIRL

FIRST PART
ROBERT AND MONICA

Six years ago

We are in spring, the schoolchildren anxiously await the arrival of summer, of trips, of love affairs. Everyone's thoughts are not on the books, but on what they will do once the lessons are over.

In a class like many others, Monica and Robert sit at desks. They have known each other since the first year. They are friends.

SHE: Monica; 15 years; daughter of 2 farmers; dark hair, dark eyes.

Distinguishing features: beautiful; nature has been very generous to her: a splendid face, two fairytale eyes, smooth and flawless skin, a beautiful, toned and well-formed body, breasts not yet developed, but impressive for their firmness; Added to this is the fact that since she was a child she has always had the habit of getting to school on foot or by bicycle, given the poor economic situation of her parents, traveling miles and miles every day; moreover, she frequently and willingly helped her parents with work in the fields; when she could, she liked to relax by swimming in the small lake near her home. The result is a beautiful girl, who takes your breath away just to see her from afar.

She is not very good at school, she does not like to study much. On the other hand, she excels in all sports - not even boys can stand up to her.

She hopes to graduate, find an honest job to help her, find the boy of her dreams, start a family, later on; her dream, however, would be to become an established athlete. For this reason, whenever she can, she trains, runs, swims, does gymnastics alone on the field (without being able to afford a gym).

HE: Robert, 15, son of 2 university professors; brown hair, blue eyes. He inherited an extraordinary mind from his parents; He could get above average grades without studying, but his parents want the best for him: since he was a child they forced him to study 4 different languages and prevented him from having a real social life; the result is a very intelligent but shy and introverted boy; His peers often tease him for his physical appearance: not very tall, a little fat, absolutely denied for any activity that does not require just reasoning, a physique no longer exceptional, further ruined by years spent in books and in the PC. He has never had a girlfriend and he is aware that it will be difficult to find one, given his difficulties in relating to others; he has always been a bit resigned.

Your first day of school.

They are both late, they sit at the only free counter; for him it is love at first sight; he has never seen such a creature; being close to her makes him stay in the seventh heaven; however, he is aware that he can never have it. He is already preparing to see her while he is going to sit in another place, when she smiles at him and asks him to explain a formula that he has not understood: he smiles in turn and explains the formula with a disarming naturalness.

They become friends; Monica sees in him a tender and sensitive boy, a friend; a kind of tacit agreement is created between them; Robert becomes a kind of school "tutor" and does not skimp on trying to get her to learn the most difficult subjects: for him, having her around is a dream.

They often meet in the evenings to study together.

Monica, in her naivety, does not realize the feeling that Robert feels; on the other hand, all the boys look at her in a certain way, and he, being more reserved, does not let out what he feels; sees him as a friend and that's it.

Robert, on the other hand, over time, begins to curse himself: tell her what he feels and run the risk of losing her permanently or continue having her like this?

Graduation time - three years ago

Monica has become an even more beautiful girl than before: now she is more of a woman. Her femininity is most evident in her forms, her splendid face more formed. Her athletic skills have made her a complete athlete on a national level; After excelling in all of the girls' sports in high school, she became a professional gymnast; now his goal is to try to finish high school with dignity to dedicate himself completely to sports.

In this she owes a lot to Robert, who helped her a lot, often even making her copy in her class work; the fact is, she sees him happy to help her, and she sees nothing wrong with it.

In her naivety she doesn't realize the feeling he has for her.

Also because for a few days she has been dating a boy, with whom she is falling in love ... well, at least it seems that she is falling in love, the classic things that happen in adolescence. They meet in the evenings and on weekends, but it's not official yet. The attraction between them is strong, they almost always make love, there is a strong understanding.

She hasn't seen Robert often lately, he's quite advanced in his studies now, he doesn't need him anymore; And then it's getting boring

Robert grew up, especially in scholasticism. He has won several scholarships, especially in the fields of information technology, electronics, and programming.

Many prestigious companies are already evaluating you for interviews and job offers.

He is a genius, he succeeds very well in everything there is to think about.

But he is sad.

His abilities fail to impress the woman of his dreams, who has now become an obsession. In a desperate attempt to score points, he signed up for the city's soccer team, hoping he could get closer to Monica's interests ... with disastrous results. He left the team and mocked Felix, the captain.

He is resigned to the idea of losing her, since she is learning to study on her own and, above all, will enter the world of sports to leave hers.

Sometimes you find yourself being persistent with her:

"Are you sure you don't want me to give you a hand for your geometry test? Really, I think you need a hand, everyone has a hard time ..."

She silences him "listen, don't insist, that's enough for me alone, and I'm also learning, thank you, but don't insist."

These are now common conversations between the two of you.

Two years ago

Monica doesn't like to study, especially at the end of May. He prefers to swim, walk ...

Robert knows he should give up, but the obsession is stronger than him.

You can't help but search the Internet for all the photos of her downloaded from athletic articles, she has created her own personal folder.

There is a very closely preserved photo from an article on regional championships, in which she is portrayed in all her glory, wrapped in a tight suit that leaves little to the imagination, taken during a bodyweight exercise, while doing some kind of bridge, highlighting your shapes and muscles.

This cannot continue.

You have to go to her and talk to her, express what you feel.

You decide to call her, to make an appointment, you absolutely must talk to her:

...

Monica: "but I'm sorry if it's so important, tell me something on the phone"

Robert: "Well, saying it over the phone is embarrassing, let's say it's about the two of us, here I am ..."

Monica: What !? Both of us? Listen Robert, you and I are friends, nothing more, if that's what you wanted to tell me, avoid coming!

... you ... you ... you ... you ...

She is visibly upset, she is busy that night and cannot understand the fact that Robert has been by her side all this time with ulterior motives; And then lately he's gotten too pushy

Robert is destroyed.

Now he knows that he has also lost her as a friend.

He does not give up, decides to go to her for clarification, at least he wants me to talk to him again.

You know the path, only that it seems very short, compared to the usual: what will you say? How will the speech begin? Now you have guessed the truth and lost it forever. How can it be remedied?

As he approaches the entrance of the house, he hears a stream of water in the pond adjacent to Monica's house.

Robert knows that he loves to swim in the afternoon to keep fit.

She is stronger than him, instead of knocking on the door, he approaches the pond, with the intention of knocking on her.

"Monica ..."

You can't hear it, it's underwater.

While swimming, Robert manages to see her in all her beauty; her body appears to be made of marble, but retains an incredible sinuosity and femininity. It moves on the water with grace and power at the same time.

At that moment he is among the trees and, when he is about to call her again, he sees her come out of the water ...

His voice hangs in his throat.

I've never seen that.

She is naked.

He approaches the shore, comes out in all its splendor, the drops of water draw beautiful paths all over his body, while he comes out and twists his hair. The full but firm breasts move sinuously along with the pectoral muscles; In the abdomen, the sculpted abs from years of exercise stand out. The legs are sharp, long, but also defined and muscular. His body is a hymn to perfection. When he approaches the shore, Robert sees all his nakedness and remains motionless without being able to make a sound.

But something unexpected happens.

She is not alone.

Robert hears laughter behind a bush where Monica is heading.

Now he's lost sight of her, but he can hear laughter, moans of pleasure, and more laughter.

"Monica, I think you should speak clearly with Robert, tell him that we are together and stop cheating on him, a girl like you would make anyone fall in love ..."

"But I didn't think he had ulterior motives ... it's ... it's just lately that he's become insistent, inexplicably jealous, possessive, this is giving me a lot of trouble ... I ... I don't know how to tell him, he doesn't seem understand. Maybe I should have known a long time ago. "

"It is better to clarify as soon as possible, if you do not do it I will"

"Don't worry, are you jealous? How could I feel anything for him? At first I at least thought he was kind, friendly, but now I think I understand his true intentions; and then physically ... here ... he's repulsive. ... certainly not like you ... "

They both laugh.

They stop talking and start kissing and hugging again.

Robert is simply petrified.

After all these years that he has been close to her ...

Those words chill him.

You would like to shout your anger and frustration to the whole world, but it would be inconvenient to make yourself heard at that moment.

The most logical thing is to walk away in silence, and it is a decision that is almost clear in the mind.

Going up the shore, with many difficulties, he looks for a path less steep than before; as he does so, he trips over a branch with the resulting thud.

"Oh my, did you hear that Monica?"

"I guess so! Who could it be? Has someone come to spy on us?"

They dress as little as possible and wander through the trees in search of the intruder.

Robert is on the run, at this point he starts to run stealthily, but the man is on him in seconds.

He recognizes, in the gloom, the captain of the school football team.

Felix.

"Robert?"

"What? Don't tell me you came here to spy on us!"

"... nn ... no ... please guys, it's not how you think, Monica ... I ... I came here just to talk to you, I heard a noise and I came to the lake, you didn't hear me, but I called you ... "

A punch to the jaw cuts him off abruptly.

"You are some kind of useless worm, now I will teach you to come spy on MY girlfriend"

"... no, Felix, please ..."

A knee to the stomach silences him even more.

Robert is on the ground, helpless.

But more than the physical pain it is the excruciating humiliation that he is suffering that makes him suffer.

Monica takes Felix's hand before she hits him again.

"Stop, Felix!"

Robert has a breather. Perhaps Monica wants to listen to him, aware of all the afternoons we spent together.

Nothing is further from reality.

She walks up to him, half naked, in her underwear and a light tank top still wet for the bathroom.

The contrast between her, tall, pretty, strong, of a healthy color, a little tanned ... and him, on the floor, hunched over himself, thin shoulders and arms, a belly growing around the waist, a consequence of years stands out. past, studying.

She is above him and sees her as an angel to his rescue.

A dream vision, he is fantasizing about kissing her, running his hands over that fantastic body, lying on a deserted beach, with her forever.

Monica brings him back to reality. She lifts him up with one hand by his shirt, looks him straight in the eye.

"Felix, it's useless to get your hands dirty with this nothing, hitting him would only end in trouble. As for you, subspecies of mollusk, never speak to me again, I was so naive to think that you were close to me amicably, but I would have fact I had to have understood immediately what all your insistence was made of, jealousy, obsession; Print this voice and this face well in your mind, because you will never speak to me again. Thank God I will leave next week, to go to a place where I hope there is no one willing to offer me help "disinterestedly" and then spy on me in my privacy ".

Will disappear.

"Let's go home, Felix. "

Robert on the ground, unable to look back, in a shower of tears, crawls home.

The physical pain is hardly felt.

SECOND PART
SONIA AND MONICA

31

3 years ago

Her: Sonia, 18 years old, her father works as an employee, her mother is a molecular biology teacher. Two good people. She is not beautiful. Petite, pale, it doesn't matter much, it's feminine enough but it's certainly not provocative. She is an intelligent girl, inherited from her mother a great passion for biology and genetics.

Very reserved and demure, she has never had boys, not so much because of her physical appearance, not exuberant but not reprehensible, but because she is NOT interested in boys.

His interests are limited to reading, research, genetics. A cold, calculating and unsociable girl.

And of a subtle, innate and inexplicable sadism.

It often happens that he goes to the laboratory, secretly from his mother, to look for an animal and torture it for no precise reason. He likes that feeling of power over the victim and seeing the unsuccessful attempt to escape his destiny on the part of the strongest specimens.

And thanks to his ability to measure his cruelty, he has never killed anyone.

Your favorite victims are the most vital and resilient, so you can try harder without permanent consequences.

In this sense, she never thought that she could torture any human specimen, even though the idea tempts her greatly.

Until that day.

We are in April two years ago.

Sonia reluctantly prepares to follow the gymnastics lesson with her classmates.

Deadly boredom, plus considerable effort.

On warm-up laps in the gym, he always falls behind along with Robert, the school's know-it-all. From time to time they talk to each other, they exchange two words talking about this and that. Clearly, they do not feel any kind of mutual attraction, they only keep company during gym hours.

She finds him very intelligent and agrees with him in many aspects of everyday life.

There is only one thing that he does not understand the meaning: the feeling he has for Monica, that gymnastic, arrogant, stupid and, above all, insensitive, seen as "exploiting" poor Robert. He doesn't understand how a smart guy can be teased like that and at the same time be persistent and stubborn in his obsession.

His is pure contempt.

However, there is something that confuses his feelings: Monica's body. Is it possible that nature is so mocking as to lock such a superficial, insensitive, and stupid person in such a perfect shell?

Sometimes in the locker room, she realizes that he is looking at her longer than he should, but she doesn't understand why.

That stupid gym hour is about to end, just waiting for the last exercise on the pole and then going to do the test in biology class, which will be over in ten minutes, by the usual genius Robert, and then all the others, who it will take a little longer.

It was that little bitch Monica who insisted she wanted to climb the pole, cheered aloud by everyone else, of course.

As Sonia prepares to try in vain to climb, Mónica involuntarily hits her, causing her to bang her nose against the post, with a general laugh.

"Hush guys, come on, do this exercise quick, we're already late ..."

"I'm sorry ..." Monica says, and with an almost animal lightness she climbs to the top and then descends just as quickly.

"I'm sorry, you damn fool" ... that's what Sonia is thinking, but she's just thinking. As she clings to the pole pretending a futile effort to climb, she observes Monica on the adjoining pole: white T-shirt, dark shorts (as in the school uniform), visible panties and bra. As part of the shorts goes up, it falls due to contact with the stick, exposing a black thong and part of her whitish buttocks that contract with effort. On the way down, however, it is the shirt that is lifted, exposing the navel and flat abdomen. The moment he steps down from the pole, he makes the gesture of lifting his shirt to dry his face, showing the perfection of his abdomen.

At that precise moment, Sonia sees herself in her laboratory with her instruments and Monica half-naked, sweaty and panting, immobilized on a table with cords and straps of all kinds, while she waits for her to do her work trying to squirm in various ways like a laboratory animal ... "excuses are not enough, you disgusting bitch, now I teach you education".

She had heard about orgasm from her companions and, in fact, she had lightly stroked herself, feeling a subtle pleasure.

But in that moment, imagining that scene, while she was clinging to the pole, gives him devastating pleasure, as if he had to restrain himself to avoid screaming.

Since that day his life has changed, he sees Monica as a potential victim of his fantasies and he takes pleasure in it.

Animals are no longer enough.

A few weeks later.

How stupid Sonia feels.

Her obsession with Monica had deprived her of clarity.

She should have imagined that no one would please her with their wicked games.

And he shouldn't have invited Monica to his house.

On the other hand, he did not resist. In the bathrooms after class, he found her in front of her for the umpteenth time, and this time naked, while she was showering.

While Monica was soaping with her eyes closed, Sonia's ate that body in every inch, envying for a moment that sponge with which she used to wash.

As the fantasy ran through his head, the other girls noticed Sonia's fixation and snickered.

They were left alone after five minutes.

Monica: "Why are you taking so long? I thought I was the only one who loved a long shower ..."

"... how? Oh yeah ... well it's relaxing."

He was about to go off and turn off the taps.

"Hey Monica, you got some soap left on your butt"

"Uh thanks! What a spirit of observation! Now I am leaving that tonight I have the cross country race, if I also win with the boys I will set a new record, you know?"

"Hey, you're very athletic, as well as pretty"

"Thank you" he smiles, he does not imagine malice on the part of many men, much less a woman.

"By the way, do you know that many athletes use electrostimulation? Do you use it?

"Well, not for now, although I've heard of it; I don't know much about it."

"Really? Do you want to come see me? I have some devices, for biology studies, you know. I can let you try them ..."

She had gone to his house.

Like two friends.

Sonia did not dare to tell him that she used those tools for her sadistic games with laboratory animals.

They had locked themselves in the room.

"Now. Undress ..."

"Sorry?"

Sonia was not very sociable and did not understand that a few circumstantial words are usually in good taste, before getting to the point.

"Well ... well ... weren't you here to try the electrostimulators? I have to apply them all over the place. You can stay in your underwear and bra if you want."

Monica, a bit annoyed, started to undress, since she basically came for that, so she did not create a fuss.

Sonia had almost lost control when she lifted her shirt. With almost haunted eyes, he stared at his new lab guinea pig.

"... listen, I did a thirty kilometer run yesterday, I'm a little tired, maybe we couldn't try those things of yours first just somewhere and then see if it hurts?"

Thirty kilometers and she's a bit tired, Sonia thought; a perfect athlete; in this specimen I can test everything and more ... and already his mind was lost in the idea of everything he could test in a woman like this: fatigue tests, prolonged stimulations of pleasure mixed with pain, threshold controls, pain ...

She was interrupted in her thoughts by Monica who saw her as in a trance

"Hey hi! Sonia, are you here with me?"

"oh yeah sure, let's try it ... on the buttocks, okay"

"Buah ... On the buttocks?"

"Why? Are you embarrassed? Can I help you ..."

After putting plenty of gel on the electrodes, he arranged them very carefully, almost maniacally, on the buttocks and part of the inner thigh.

It did not seem real to Sonia that she could touch this animal with impunity, and she had to refrain from lingering too long on its flesh to avoid making her suspicious. But the position in which she had been placed, legs apart, slightly bent forward, with one hand holding her hair still and the other resting on the bedside table, in her underwear, made it impossible not to test the firmness of her buttocks and the inner thigh.

Monica noticed this and seemed a bit upset.

Then Sonia pulled herself together.

"Ok, now I'm sending you 1 second pulses at level 1"

Monica felt a tingle, but nothing moved.

Then Sonia went straight to level 3.

Monica felt her muscles contract every second; It initially took her by surprise, then she began to find it almost pleasant.

Sonia saw her glutes and adductors contract and began to go into crisis. He would have liked to stun her, strip her of what little she had left, tie her up well and progressively reach level 10 throughout her body.

But it was a fantasy.

He almost collapsed when he barely heard a moan at the moment of contraction.

Was it possible that she liked him?

Unless...

He got the unhealthy idea ...

"Listen, since I think you're liking it, can we try it on the whole body?"

"Ah well yes, ok"

The placement of the electrodes lasted more than ten minutes.

Sonia wanted to enjoy every moment that that beautiful body touched.

He had put electrodes everywhere.

The smallest in biceps, triceps, calves.

Those a little bigger in abdomen, back, pectorals, thighs, in addition to the ones I already had.

With an unbelievable excuse, saying he had to connect "equipment ground," he effectively pinned her to a frame that was used as a hanger in the laboratory.

And he had also removed her bra saying "just to be safe" she had to place sensors in that area for the heartbeat. In this way she wrapped her nipples with special electrodes and secured the breast part to the frame.

The result was Monica tied up in an X shape, with a practically naked body if not for her little black thong, and the electrodes attached to most of her body, front and back.

"... but ... but ... I can't move"

"This way I can put the electrodes where I want, and with stretched arms and legs your muscles will work better"

Monica didn't understand much and it seemed very strange, but she trusted that.

All the electrodes were connected to a machine that Sonia manipulated with expert hands.

It started with levels 3 and 4.

Enraptured by this living work of art, she dosed the levels and intervals at will, admiring how all of Monica's muscles were practically at her service.

Monica found this a little strange, but the physical sensation was pleasant.

However, there was something that disturbed her in Sonia's eyes, she seemed almost ecstatic.

"Well, interesting, Sonia." I didn't ask you how long these sessions usually last. No, I'm telling you because I have a date tonight and I don't want ...

She was silenced by a gag that Sonia, in the midst of ecstasy, put it violently into her mouth, immobilizing her even more against the structure.

"Shut up bitch!"

Monica, almost incredulous, tried to free herself, but to no avail. From the gag she emitted almost animal sounds, of uncontrolled rage, when Sonia approached her.

He began to lick her, kiss her, nibble on every point of her body.

And what excited her most were the outbursts of rebellion and revulsion in her guinea pig.

For the next five minutes, he raised the level to 7 and saw her muscles contract unnaturally, and the sweat further increased the conductivity of the electrodes.

Monica went from a mood first to incredulous anger, then to panic, and finally ... almost to arousal. How was it possible to get turned on by such a depraved woman? Furthermore, his body in violent spasms told him otherwise.

Sonia had noticed that the thong had gotten wet and was smiling devilishly. He came over and began to play with the thong in order to remove it.

However, Monica absolutely wanted to get out of that situation desperately and reason prevailed.

With an incredible effort he managed to break part of the metal structure and free his right hand.

Then he removed the gag and began to scream with the breath possible in his throat, ripping off all the electrodes.

Sonia found her in front of her free and received a kick in the face that made her faint.

Monica, in a panic, fled with her clothes.

In a moment of clarity, he thought of alerting the police once he got home.

Now Sonia and Monica are at the police station.

Monica had sued Sonia for sexual assault, telling the truth in every detail. However, Sonia's house was isolated and no one had seen her leave in that state nor had anyone heard her scream. In addition, the story was not very credible, because the police found it strange that a strong woman like her was immobilized by a thin one like Sonia. And then the "treatment" had left no mark on his body, which was now in perfect health.

Sonia was cursing herself.

What had occurred to him?

Attack her like this.

It was certainly a dream to have her, even for a few minutes, but now?

Monica will never trust her again.

The mockery of the companions and the opinions of the people did not interest him. What bothered her the most was having lost control and been thrown into a dangerous situation.

He certainly couldn't have predicted that the raging beast would break part of the metal frame, but with such a physique ...

She promised herself that in the future she would be a thousand times more careful. Because she's still determined to make her fantasy come true.

For the moment, she limits herself to handling the unpleasant situation: in the absence of evidence, it is she who accuses Monica of having attacked her with a kick after having almost undressed her to seduce her. The version of Sonia, with her appearance of the typical girl with good manners, and from a good family, sustained by the wound on the lip caused by Monica's kick, is more likely in the eyes of the police who hypothesize an attack by Monica after a refusal from Sonia.

After several days of investigations, people questioned, everything ends in a stalemate due to lack of evidence.

Sonia lets out a liberating sigh of relief within herself; after assuming a scared and indignant expression in front of the commissioners. Once outside, he looks Monica directly in the eyes with an evil and lustful smile as if to say: Did you see, stupid whore, what am I capable of? In his eyes, you are almost more guilty than me. Know that sooner or later you will be MIA ...

Monica is puzzled.

He realizes that he has acted naively and recklessly.

Just a few days ago, she discovered that Robert, her fellow student, had ulterior motives and came to spy on her while she was intimate with Felix.

And now this classmate immobilizes her to torture her. Luckily he had the strength to free himself, otherwise ... try not to think about what might have happened. Besides that state of excitement when she was helpless at the mercy of that madwoman?

Better not think about it and think about your future as an athlete, going back to training.

And without electrostimulators ...

Small parenthesis

One week after the fact.

Monica shared her version with her classmates / friends. Many people believe Monica, she is a very loved and respected girl, not only an object of envy and desire.

Sonia has no friends, she is a shy girl. As a result, he does not care about people's disparaging looks. He went back to playing his little games with laboratory animals and guinea pigs.

Today a day trip to the park is planned.

She will be alone watching the boys and girls joke around, play games and court each other, including Monica.

Curiously that day, after swimming in the lake in the park, a group of girls began to meet with her, to talk about this and that.

Together they go for a walk in the woods.

When they get near a noisy waterfall, they stop talking.

Sonia is frightened by the look of her unlikely friends.

"Now you will have a little lesson"

She is carried on the wings, unable to rebel, behind a rock, scared.

Monica is waiting for her behind the rock.

"It's all yours, Monica, give her a good lesson, we will stay at the entrance to prevent anyone from approaching, although the place is almost unknown; in about twenty minutes we will come back for you; have fun."

Sonia is in a state of terror.

The imposing and beautiful figure of the object of her wishes stands out one meter from her. But it is not what you would like. Sonia would like to have her tied up, at his mercy, now they are alone and only God knows what will happen.

Monica takes off her shorts and T-shirt, staying in a bikini.

He approaches Sonia, who for a moment sees her as a lover and falls to his knees to admire her.

When he sees Monica like this he no longer thinks, he makes the gesture of kissing her navel.

In response, he receives a kick to the stomach.

"Now get naked, BITCH"

Without understanding his intentions, he obeys without hesitation.

"Completely"

Monica also takes off her latest clothes.

"Don't get weird ideas, bitch, I don't want to get my clothes wet"

The two girls, naked, are an obvious contrast between them; beauty and ugliness, strength and fragility, exuberant sensuality and shameful shyness.

Monica drags her by the hair towards the waterfall and throws her into the water, diving after her.

He takes her by the neck and lifts her up.

"Now in these twenty minutes I will have a little revenge, bitch, and I hope, especially for you, that you never speak to me again ... ah, don't worry, I will not leave visible signs for you to report me"

Sonia looks at her former guinea pig with nostalgia and admiration.

As she is bent over with her hands around her neck, her eyes are full of anger. In the effort to lift her, he contracts every muscle in his magnificent body.

Sonia sees Monica in all her splendor and in all her fury, even if the situation is reversed, compared to last time.

During the next 20 minutes, Monica dunks Sonia's head several times, pushing her to the limit. While holding it, he also hits it a few times. You must vent your anger at having suffered that feeling of vulnerability that you felt in the house of the whore. And above all because of that senseless excitement he had felt.

Even at this moment he wonders why he had to completely undress, the swimsuit would have dried in the heat.

And by being naked and alone with that perverse being, she becomes excited again.

This infuriates her even more, causing her to hold her head underwater for a few moments longer than she should.

Sonia gulps water and begins to cough convulsively.

Monica stops, gathering herself.

In these minutes Sonia suffers physically, but clearly she knows that Monica just wants to teach her a lesson. And this reassures her. And seeing that beast in all its fury turns her on, thinking about what it might do to him, if he's in the right condition.

"Now go away"

Monica says, a little shocked by the inexplicable emotion she felt just before.

Sonia looks at her, dressing, wondering if Monica's nipples are so erect because of the cold water or for other reasons.

The eyes meet and Sonia once again has that diabolical light in her eyes.

-I want to have it-

Monica thinks of Sonia.

She leaves, coughing, shooting murderous looks at the "friends" on duty.

Monica knows that her friends join her when she yells at them.

"Leave her alone!"

The friends understand the difficult moment and withdraw.

In the solitude of the waterfall, Monica finds herself grappling with her instincts.

She is naked in the water; In recent times, events with Robert and Sonia are making him understand how much their shocking beauty affects people.

He almost feels guilty.

And uncomfortable.

She feels observed.

He turns towards the top of the waterfall.

A stealthy shadow flees and retreats into a bush.

Monica, still shocked by what happened, with a prodigious jump quickly reaches the bush at the top of the waterfall and manages to catch the unsuspecting "admirer" ... Robert.

"How? You again?"

Monica is in awe of how much more and more she is the object of unwanted attention.

Robert has nothing to say, this time he knows he is wrong and it is completely unjustifiable.

Monica, in the midst of an uncontrolled rage, hits him with two fists and squeezes his neck with force.

"Damn it! Can you know what you want from me? I just want you to leave me alone. Wasn't the lake lesson enough for you?"

Robert, unable to react, is on the ground. His beloved's hands are clutching his neck as she sits on top of him, naked astride him. Despite the dangerous situation, seeing that wild beauty, he can't help but stretch his hands over Monica's naked body, get turned on, now he has nothing to lose.

Monica barely understands the situation, and when she notices an unmistakable bulge in the boy's boxers, repelled by the appearance of the individual, she gives him a firm kick in the lower parts, causing him indescribable pain.

The situation of her naked on a boy on the floor, combined with the events from just before, again provokes a strange excitement in the girl, almost fascinated by her power and strength, and by the effect she has on people.

Forcefully pushing the thought out of his mind, he flees leaving a physically annihilated Robert on the ground.

What just happened to him, that violent kick, is causing excruciating pain in his lower parts.

The object of his desire is increasingly unattainable for him, and he falls lower and lower

Lately he had found out what happened between Sonia and his object of desire.

This bothers him a lot. Above all, he wonders how Sonia managed to convince Monica to freeze like this. Then the story of electrostimulators ... he gets ashamed of himself by getting aroused just thinking about it.

He feels some envy for that strange slim and ugly girl with a passion for genetics: he thought he had her, if only for a few minutes and in a wicked way.

And how much would he have given to be alone with her in that house, with her completely naked and tied up?

But what is he thinking about? No, thinking about these things will only hurt you.

Worthy resignation is better.

THIRD PART
MONICA AND HER COSTUME

2018 - The sport

No one who has seen Monica in recent years, her body, what she is capable of, even in competition with the guys, would have the slightest doubt that she has all the credentials to become an absolute level athlete. It almost seems, at 21, that he exceeds the laws of physics at times. What is surprising about her is the fact that she excels both in disciplines where strength is required (such as shot put, javelin throw) and in speed disciplines such as running; She manages to get ahead of black athletes in purely speed disciplines, causing amazement, admiration and even envy from the athletes around her.

Swimming allows him to stay in shape, but even in this discipline he excels and manages to keep up with most of the boys.

The discipline in which he manages to combine everything with exceptional results is pole vault, so much so that he focuses more on that specialty, with a bit of regret for not being able to compete in all disciplines (which he could easily do).

Her relationship with Felix ended a long time ago, despite the attraction she felt, she could not bear his jealousy; on the other hand, she understands, seeing herself in the mirror, that no man can stop admiring her. But it's better this way, at that moment she feels good about herself and free.

Only from a professional point of view is something missing. It is true that she is preparing for the Olympic Games, which is already quite famous, that she has been proposed to walk, pose for calendars ... yet she feels almost trapped by that life of training and racing.

Would like to have more satisfaction.

The birth of the superhero

On a Sunday like any other, after spending a Saturday at a disco with friends and a wonderful night of love with a boy she met that same night, she watches television and is intrigued by a series in which three beautiful girls dress up in a tight suit and ... they steal.

Monica has no financial problems, although she does not sail in gold, but her desire to try new emotions prevails.

One night she dons a tight dark gray bathing suit.

You wear it with nothing underneath.

Also prepare a face covering, which is also tight-fitting.

Your first "mission" is to explore the city.

How to do it without being seen?

His athletic abilities come to his aid ... and so does his axis.

From the window of the residence, at 2 in the morning, she comes down silently without being discovered, also helped by the color of the suit.

Although he cannot be seen well like this, he decides to cross the less crowded areas.

Roofs are the easiest places to get everything under control.

Monica is satisfied with herself: the idea of jumping from ceiling to ceiling with the help of a pole, in addition to allowing her to have the situation under control, allows her to train even more (as if she needed it).

After the first night of patrol, more come, but so far it seems more like a game.

One night he realizes that a group of criminals is breaking into a supermarket.

Common sense tells you to warn the authorities ... but your courage prevails.

With a prodigious jump he lands on the roof of the supermarket.

He sneaks down through a window to watch four men in ski masks empty boxes.

She doesn't know why she got in there, what can she do now? Maybe just curiosity or the desire to test yourself.

His movements are helped by the fact that the lights are off and the criminals are not aware of his presence. But something unexpected happens: the one who seems to be the boss says something to his partner, who goes to the dashboard turning on all the lights: he has obviously noticed his presence.

With her heart in her throat, Monica crouches behind the refrigerated counter, trying to quickly win the exit.

One of the four sees it!

"Hey, you stop ..."

Monica tries to escape from the man and she is succeeding, being very fast; She decides to go back to the window through which she entered, she has already placed several meters between her and the man, when around a corner she meets the boss and another, both with a gun pointed at her.

"Game over"

Now there are four around her and Monica curses herself for her recklessness and stupidity.

"Now tell me who you are and what are you doing here, meanwhile, with your hands on your head"

Now that Monica is with her hands above her head, the tight jumpsuit highlights her sinuous forms, her plump and firm breasts, her sculpted buttocks, her muscular arms, the fact that she is afraid, more than the fatigue of running, makes her breathing fast and short of breath. Feel the bullies' eyes on her.

"You're a woman, huh? Interesting, now while I'm pointing this gun at you, take off that cute costume, start with your face, I want to see you in the face"

Monica does not know what to do ... the thieves have ski masks, the cameras are not a problem for them, but she ... her recognized face, her photo in the newspapers, her ruined career, the ridicule of people ... is petrified and unable to think clearly.

"Well at this point ... you two, hold her tight."

The two approach her and take her arms, keeping them firmly behind her back; she fears the worst.

"Boss, she's a little taller than us, and look at her arms ... wouldn't it be better to tie her up?"

"Enough, remember that there are four of us and that she is just a woman, coward"

The chief approaches with the pistol pointed and gestures to remove the mask.

Monica, at this point, following her instinct, stretches a strong knee towards the lower parts of the man, throws with force the two who were holding her against the wall, taking them off her like two twigs. Then he grabs the boss's sore head and throws it against the wall towards the room that was pointing the gun at him.

With a jump he is on both of them, he takes the weapons and pushes them, beginning to hit and kick the unfortunate two, making them pass out.

The remaining two, the ones holding her arms, throw themselves at her with two iron bars. The first is neutralized by a kick to the nose, but the second manages to hit Monica in the abdomen; incredulous he sees that the girl feels the blow and collapses for a moment, but in a second she is on her feet and disarms him. Now he is the only one who is not unconscious, but is terrified: who could get back on his feet after such a blow?

Monica grabs him by the neck and slams him against a wall. She herself is fascinated by his strength and power. She remembers the situation, the feeling with her back to the wall, with four men against her, two of whom are armed, their greedy glances towards her gray suit, the awareness of being victorious, they excite her again ... the same emotion that had troubled her a few years ago. The thing bothers her, she squeezes the victim's neck hard ...

Sirens interrupt everything.

Monica realizes the danger of being discovered and quickly escapes.

"Wait ... but who is it, that thing dressed in gray, it looked like a woman ... guys, come here, there are four unconscious robbers on the ground, check it out."

Monica is very fast, adrenaline helps her.

Reached the ceiling, use the pole to jump from one to the other, the sound of the sirens fades.

Upon reaching a sparsely populated area, he descends from the rooftops and begins running at breakneck speed, stick in hand, toward the residence.

Miraculously she is not discovered and falls into her room with great relief.

She's a little shocked, but she's okay.

But what happens to her?

He wants to understand.

She goes to the mirror, takes off her mask, she's still in disguise.

He also takes off his gray suit and looks at his naked body; she is sweaty from running. Her memories fly to her first "patrol", then to the encounter with the thieves, the weapons pointed at her, her devastating reaction ... and a few years ago again ... that wicked girl who immobilizes and tortures her. And see the one forcibly released ... the one holding the girl's head underwater, the one beating up "voyeur" Robert.

It is observed as her hand goes to caress itself, rolls on the floor, squeezes her breasts hard ... and achieves a pleasure never experienced before.

She is upset.

Not even happy.

But he liked walking around the city at night ...

The day after the news and newspapers talk about the story, a video in which, dressed in gray, she throws herself on the criminals and flees is shown repeatedly on various stations and on the internet.

"The thieves, when questioned, reveal how this" gray ghost "came out of nowhere and how his extraordinary strength allowed him to knock them out ... now people are already cheering on an unlikely superhero" 'Fantastic Girl', is the name more popular ... who is it? Why does he do this? How can it be so strong? All the questions that, at the moment, have no answer ... "

Reading the article, Monica smiles, knowing they can't trace it back to her.

Fantastic Girl likes ...

Of course the police will look for her, she is still someone who does not respect the laws, going down the windows of supermarkets at night and taking justice on her own ...

He decides to wait a few weeks before "going out" again.

December 2018 - The Capture

It's been a few months since Fantastic Girl was born.

Monica is amazed that an external committee on campus has brought together a series of 16- to 35-year-old girls, of great physical strength, more or less of the same height and complexion.

The appointment is on the athletics field, where a line of girls is made so that one by one they enter and sit in a room, exchange a few words with a lady and leave immediately afterwards.

Monica is perplexed, but quietly enters the room.

A woman in her fifties is sitting in the chair with a strange cell phone on the table (she has never seen that model before).

Now he recognizes the woman since he had witnessed her interrogation for the episode with Sonia.

After observing Monica from head to toe with a strange look, he asks her information, name, address, age, etc. ...

The last question takes her by surprise:

"Do you know Fantastic Girl?"

Monica is incredulous, what kind of question is that?

After a moment of indecision:

"Well yeah, I know she's some kind of superhero who lately 'watches' the city ..."

The lady interrupts her.

"Well, yes, actually she is useful for the community, even if she is still an outlaw; that's why the police would like to question her, but she doesn't seem very inclined to be arrested; it's a shame, the police would like to collaborate with her ..."

"I understand, but why did you come here?"

"Well it's simple, the little data we have on Fantastic Girl is that she is a woman, that she is strong, tall, athletic and operates in this region ... let's say we are taking data on potential heroines, nothing to worry about. .. "

The lady looks at the cell phone.

"Are you Fantastic Girl?"

Monica hints at a fake smile.

"But let's not joke, of course not!"

The lady looks at the cell phone.

"Okay Monica, you can go."

Monica is concerned, even though they have no evidence to locate her.

In recent months she has always been cautious.

His patrols were very discreet, only when he encountered something serious, such as muggings, robberies, violence, did he intervene quickly and lethally: he does not remember how many robbers, rapists and robbers he had knocked out with relative ease.

Several times she ran into the police, whose aim was, however, to arrest her, but she quickly fled.

In any case, the policemen pursued her as a way of speaking, more out of duty; after all, one like that in the city was convenient for them. For this reason it seems even more strange that some "outside commission" bothers to understand who Fantastic Girl is.

And then that lady seemed very, too sure of herself.

Well, in any case she would never have given up on that life: there was too much satisfaction, too much adrenaline every time she put on that costume.

In recent months he has notably intensified his training, improving even more (as if necessary) his strength and, above all, his elasticity.

He didn't know that his body could go this far, he had discovered more hidden potential, developed muscles in areas he never imagined.

And when she quietly descended from the roofs of houses to surprise criminals and knock them out, even though prudence suggested otherwise, she always preferred to be discovered, then to show her strength and knock out four or five at the same time. The amazement of the unfortunate, their fear and the awareness of their power caused him strange sensations, similar to those he hated when he was with Sonia or Robert.

Tonight was like any other.

Thieves in a shopping center.

There is no shadow of a police patrol.

It is their moment.

He enters and, in the dark, sees seven armed men.

This time it will be difficult, but he has already brought down more of them with his extraordinary strength and agility.

And so it happens.

Appearing out of nowhere, he catches the seven men off guard and knocks them out with ease.

But he hadn't seen the eighth, who had seen the scene from above.

A dart sticks in his arm; no one had ever hit her. After two seconds you are already unconscious.

That night the cops don't seem to give credit that they "caught" Fantastic Girl, so much so that they are already discussing the possibility of not revealing that she was already unconscious on the ground to take credit and go as heroes.

In any case, they handcuff her and take her to the cell, waiting to be interrogated the next day.

Monica wakes up in her cell, handcuffed, in her costume and ... without a mask.

She is furious, but with herself. Too confident and light in acting, too confident in his gymnastic qualities.

Now her identity will be revealed to the press and, sadly, many things will change for her.

I could hear the guards arguing.

"After the photos of Fantastic Girl are published, the press will spread the story of how we captured her; I already called a journalist friend, the photos are in the archive. I feel a little sorry for her; but in the meantime after what that she did for the city, no judge will have the courage to sentence her, not even to pay a fine. The only thing is that now everyone knows who she is. Monica G. is Fantastic Girl, who would have thought? Sure, now we explain physical strength ...

Hey, stop, who are you? No one can enter here ... "

A thud. A hit. Another thud.

Seven men in blue suits enter armed and open the cell, pointing strange weapons at it. A dart hits her and she passes out.

The day after in the newspapers:

"SENSATIONAL: Fantastic Girl turns out to be the promise of world athletics Monica G., considered by all almost an alien for her athletic gifts, not least for her beauty. But on the day of capture she manages to escape somehow, perhaps with the help of accomplices. The fact is that she neutralized two guards and fled. No one finds her, she did not appear for training. The police have already issued the border alert. The truth is that, before she was a heroine loved by all, after killing two officers is guilty of murder ... "

FOURTH PART
ROBERT AND SONIA

2018 - Career, complicity

Who hasn't fantasized about being a CIA agent?

In the collective imagination, it is they who are decisive for events of vital importance such as terrorism, attempted attacks, etc.

In the movies, for example, you don't even need to talk about that anymore.

Agents, men or women prepared for anything, more physically and intellectually gifted than others, morally inflexible and loyal to their homeland.

Unfortunately (or fortunately, depending on your point of view) things are very different in the real world.

The "group", in the first place, has no name and is not known to ordinary people.

Sure, the CIA exists, it does a lot of the activities you see in the movies.

But whoever really controls everything cannot be there for all to see.

And whoever works there is anything but morally incorruptible, indeed, the opposite is sought.

But let's take a few steps back.

2017 - Recruitment

Sonia is not depressed, she is "on hold", waiting for a favorable situation.

After the nonsense with Monica, people, unlike with the famous athlete in the city, avoid her.

Not a day goes by without cursing that damn Thursday he decided to invite Monica.

Of course, that day he also experienced the greatest emotion of his life ...

Given the discrimination she suffered, she also had to struggle to find work; that is why she is amazed by the interview given in a conference room of the best hotel in the city; he does not know what it is or the name of the company.

"Good morning Sonia"

"Hello".

A woman in her fifties greets her confidently, with a strange light in her eyes.

"How does it feel to be considered a perverse sadistic lesbian by the citizens?"

"I ... I don't ..."

"Oh, Sonia, it's useless to deny it. Look, I was present at the time of the complaint, when I found out about the nature of the complaint I ran to this city and attended your interrogation. Look, you were very clever in denying and inventing that story. that YOU rejected Monica and she hit you. But I had this ... "

An object similar to a mobile phone.

"See, this object indicates without the possibility of error if a person is lying or not ... and Monica was not lying, I assure you"

Sonia was angry.

"Look, I don't know what he wants from me, these miserable deceptions leave me indifferent; his story doesn't even hold up; if it was as he says he would have had to intervene and arrest me after questioning, instead of dropping the matter for lack of evidence "

"And why would I have to?"

"But ... I'm sorry, isn't it from the police? What do you want from me?"

"Make yourself comfortable, girl, now I'll tell you who I am and what I want; I'm very interested in your knowledge of genetics, by the way ... ah, tell me about yourself"

In about thirty minutes it clears everything up.

The group controls the destiny of the world. He does it with an invisible hand. The funds and facilities it owns are secret. Like the advanced technologies they have, including the "truth phone" seen above. In addition to agents scattered around the world, it has a research center divided into several departments: engineering, physics, genetics.

The Biology / Genetics Center deals with human experiments of various kinds. Thanks to the risky miscegenation, the surgery, the electroshock, the group has managed to create the perfect soldier, from the human being: they are perfectly healthy men and women who have grown since they were born in the laboratory, but with one fundamental characteristic: obedience blind to superior; devoid of different wills and desires to serve the group.

In the center there are numerous studies, always experimenting, on fatigue, resistance to pain, sexual instinct. These experiments are carried out, only for cognitive purposes and pending future developments, on unfortunate poor people.

Guinea pigs are selected with care: humans of both sexes, of legal age, healthy and robust to the extent possible to withstand various "treatments." Mainly athletes, soldiers, physically strong specimens, even prisoners or prostitutes are chosen. The lucky ones are used for reproduction and forced to mate with other "recruits" repeatedly. Others are used for fatigue tests. The most unlucky for pain threshold tests. Some particularly attractive specimens are "seized" by management and used for the pleasure of the staff.

Perfectly created soldiers are used for "recruitment", infallible soldiers who manage to carry out kidnappings masterfully. Subjects are chosen from the upper echelons of the organization, of which the mysterious woman is a part.

Center directors are aging and struggling to keep up with technology. A renovation is needed.

The management selected Sonia for two essential characteristics: biological-genetic knowledge and her lack of humanity.

"Dear Sonia, I know that now everything seems unreal to you. Know that if you are one of us you will dedicate your life to us. You will not need the salary because you will live in the structure. But the best reward will be, for you, a fully equipped area for your experiments, with so many human and modified guinea pigs at your command. I know you like that, don't be ashamed. We spied on you while you were playing your "games" with the animals. Come here at the same time tomorrow, if you are one of us. If we do not see you, it means that you are not interested and we will erase your memory of this meeting ... yes, of course we can. If you come with us you will disappear and for your acquaintances you will no longer exist. The last thing: we do not want to have the world in our hands We just want to check that no one has absolute power. This requires sacrifices,even innocent lives.

Goodbye, or rather see you soon, Sonia.

Ah, I'm member 231, ask for me "

Sonia has a sleepless night. He has already decided to accept, but he wants to enjoy his "no goodbye" to his parents, to his acquaintances, thinking about how little he cares about all of them; his only regret: will he ever get his hands on Monica again? Who knows?

In any case, it will disappear without noise ...

The next day he arrives at the appointment with a backpack full of those few useful things for a woman.

"I was hoping to see you again, Sonia. If you have clothes in your backpack I tell you that it will not be necessary, you will find everything you need in our offices"

"Okay"

"Trust me, if you behave you will be rewarded with interest ..."

Sonia does not understand the meaning of the phrase, but she gets on, without hesitation, a helicopter.

The headquarters of the research center appears to be in the middle of the sea.

Sonia almost freaks out when the helicopter descends into the open sea.

Suddenly, after a radio communication from the pilot, an island is revealed to his eyes.

Sonia is speechless.

"Cloaking devices, Sonia. The island can also be closed and submerged as a precaution when the route is crossed by a ship, but it has happened once in the last thirty-eight years ..."

An island of dreams, as big as a metropolis.

Lots of vegetation and green spaces.

An imposing structure can be seen, where the helicopter is heading.

As you zoom in, people in blue uniforms can be seen pointing strange weapons at half-naked men and women running down a fenced road at breakneck speed.

"You see, the blues are genetically modified humans; they have already received categorical approval to obey unconditionally. Right now, the guinea pigs are doing a drug resistance test to see the long-term effects of the substance; here, instead, there are the residences for the administration, of which you will be a part from today; there are only six people to manage and run the center, the rest are modified humans or guinea pigs. I give the orders to the six, I review the progress of the investigation and inform my superiors. "

Sonia meets the other six members: George and Rachel, nearing retirement, responsible respectively for the electronic / computer and biological / genetic parts (which Sonia will take care of). The other members are in charge of logistics, finances and supplies.

"Sonia, you will work alongside Rachel for a month, after which she will enjoy her well-deserved retirement and you ... your well-deserved mission."

Smile.

You already have a little practice.

The first day after "hiring" her, Sonia familiarizes herself with the procedures and equipment. Rachel kinda reminds her of herself in the way she handles guinea pigs, cold with a devilish grin.

It amazes him how all his diabolical fantasies are a simple reality in that place.

Watch in fascination as a black woman is chained to a rotating mechanism, completely naked in the sun.

The tethers are pulled so that the guinea pig is in tension. The operation is completed by modified humans; at this point Rachel intervenes.

"After the operation, as it will be reduced to a semi-vegetable state, it will be used for some other tests. It's a shame, I wish I had done it without the treatment, but it is the procedure. I would have liked to see how he reacted in all his faculties, he has a rebellious character, which I like so much. But you have to be patient.

The sea is full of fish ...

It had been selected for the test that we are carrying out this black guinea pig. Carla, is her name, a twenty-one-year-old Cuban athlete who runs 100m, 200m and also practices long jump, an athlete with great potential, as can be seen in her body. Although she still hasn't had a chance to be famous, apparently "

Sonia observes and listens with morbid attention to the nature of the test.

The guinea pig was immobilized in the sun, tied to this device that functions as a "spit." Her heart rate was monitored with electrodes Rachel had been applying to different areas and her temperature with probes placed in her vagina and anus.

In this way you can see how the guinea pig reacts to sun exposure.

The test is performed on men and women of different races and ages to obtain statistical data.

Rachel admires Nadia's body: tall, slim, muscular, without a hint of fat and, despite everything, with quite large breasts. Her hands and feet were tied in an X shape; the tension of the strings made his muscles stand out.

Of course, her features weren't pretty, not very feminine, and anyway, even as a physicist she couldn't compare to Monica ... ahhh Monica, what memories, who knows where she is now?

Sonia stops thinking about Monica and watches as Rachel coldly applies the electrodes and probes.

They are about to leave, but Sonia stays a few more minutes to observe the female naked and tied to the sun, and the operation of the mechanism that makes her turn slowly.

When the first beads of sweat form, he runs a finger under his armpits, as if to tickle Carla, who blinks, an instinctive urge to break free. The thing amuses him, so he repeats the act, touching it under his feet, on his abdomen, on his chest. It was interesting how the abs stood out even though she was "tight".

Rachel smiles.

"Come, Sonia, we have to finish today's tests, you will have time to have fun after work"

Well, she would have taken longer, she wouldn't have been in such a "rush".

In fact, she had noticed that Rachel didn't spend much time with the girls. He preferred to linger on the males, he touched them a lot, without any shame, after all, they were guinea pigs.

The day continued with regularity, Rachel explaining the work to her more and more.

At night, the guinea pigs are taken to separate cells, and fed.

The management retires to the residence, equipped with all the comforts.

Dinner served by modified humans is delicious.

Sonia fits into the group easily.

Member 231 toasts the newcomer.

"Now it's time to retire to our annexes. Well, everyone have fun as they prefer ..."

A mischievous laugh, directed at Sonia.

Rachel accompanies Sonia to the rooms.

"What did that laugh mean about fun? I don't understand ..."

"Come, Sonia, now I'll explain it to you."

He takes her to a private wing of the detention room.

"Here are the guinea pigs we have chosen for our 'entertainment'; of course they are the most attractive specimens. We can do whatever we want with them, have sex, torture them or just keep them chained in the room to admire them ".

Sonia observes about twenty cells.

The logistician, a man in his forties, fat, bald, goes to the cell of a mulatto woman. With a nod to a modified human male he enters the cell, armed.

"Tonight it's your turn, friend; strip completely"

The guinea pig, with terror in his eyes, strips naked. She is a young mulatto woman, with two beautiful green eyes. Her physique is imposing, almost two meters tall, tapered and muscular legs, firm toned and natural breasts, a fabulous body.

Sonia turns to Rachel.

"Who?"

"A twenty-two-year-old dancer. We chose her because she lived in a small town and it was very easy to pick her up; besides that she is beautiful and physically gifted, of course. Tonight it is her turn to put up with Paul: he is a sadist, he likes to use the whip. It is very good at causing pain without leaving permanent damage. In any case, the guinea pigs it "used" should rest for a few days before being reused. Observe ... "

A rectangular device that works with small wheels is introduced into the cell; the victim was tied in an X shape by the hands and feet. She cries. Obviously she knows what to expect.

Paul enters slowly examines his prey, kisses it, touches it, sniffs it.

"Smells a little, what did you make him do today?"

"Ten miles of swimming in the morning and fifty miles of running in the afternoon."

"Justly"

He takes a fire hydrant and directs it towards the guinea pig. A jet of cold water hits her violently. Then Paul soaps her thoroughly, insisting on the breasts and private parts, while she tries in vain to free herself, watching the little man with contempt and terror.

When it's all over, he rinses her off and orders the modified humans to carry the cart with the tied dancer to her room.

Rachel heads to the men's wing.

He stops in front of the cell of a muscular blond boy. This is a Swedish "partner", who had the misfortune to have Rachel as a client, who, finding him particularly attractive, persuaded Member 231 to "recruit" him.

The procedure is similar, although he is chained with his underwear still on.

Rachel invites Sonia to participate.

The boy is tall and muscular. The two women watch him like an animal. That day he underwent intensive electrostimulation treatment throughout his body.

Sonia moves behind him and runs her sharp nails down his back, causing instinctive explosions in the boy. He likes to see muscles contract with his touch. He is re-evaluating the possibility of torturing men, while still preferring women.

Rachel joins Sonia, and with expert hands they begin to tease and nibble on him from all sides.

The boy is still sweaty from the afternoon fatigue, but Rachel prefers not to wash him; he likes them when they're a little sweaty.

When the two women stand in front of him and Rachel starts to lick him on the chest, Sonia notices an unmistakable bulge in the boy's underwear.

Rachel is not a beautiful woman, in her fifties, but the elegant way she is dressed and her manipulative skills have the Swedish stud excited. Sonia, taken as if by ecstasy, excited, but at the same time indignant, gives him a violent slap and grabs him by the hair.

"How dare you, you filthy animal, get an erection? You haven't been taught good manners. Is this the way to treat a lady? Now I'll have you spanked until the urge wears off ..."

Rachel interrupts her.

"Hey, take it easy; this is MY toy, don't forget it; now I'll have it taken to my room ..."

"But ... but ... ok, sorry; it's just that I got the impression that he was having too much fun and therefore ..."

"Look, Sonia, not everyone is so sadistic. I like to tease them, torture them a little. I often like to turn them on, masturbate them to orgasm and then interrupt me immediately beforehand. You should see how they beg, I think for them it is a of the greatest humiliations. But sometimes I make them come. With whom it is worth it ... well here ... I also have relationships. Now do not be offended, but I will retire to my room with him. You can choose who you want, here the only mandatory rules are: NEVER untie them, do not permanently damage them, do not kill them.

Hey, take the Swede to my room.

Come Sonia I want to see what you choose "

Sonia walks down the aisle seeing many male specimens of various breeds, all very tall and attractive.

But his focus is on the female wing.

"Hmm ... I should have understood that he preferred women," Rachel thought smiling.

There were many girls, and very attractive; one with dark hair and eyes and a model's body vaguely reminds him of Monica, although she was more vital, stronger and more beautiful; a sadly unattainable beauty, much to Sonia's regret.

Then something comes to mind.

"Rachel, where is the Norwegian swimmer?"

"Well, she's in treatment right now, you can't take her to the room ..."

"No, here ... I'd just like to see her"

"Okay"

They walk a few floors underground and come to a room controlled by a dozen guards.

The door opens.

The Norwegian is immobilized in an X-shaped bed, with straps on ankles, thighs, waist, neck, forehead, biceps and wrists.

He has a white jumpsuit. Various threads come out of the suit in different parts of the body.

"Look, this treatment aims to make her suffer for a long time, but without causing physical harm; for this the heartbeat and temperature are monitored; if the values become critical, the electrical torture stops, leaving her to rest; there is a camera filming everything, part of the video will be broadcast to the guinea pigs as a warning.

At this moment, as I see on the computer, the guinea pig has just endured a continuous cycle of 47 minutes, as can be seen in its heavy breaths; in half an hour I should start again "

"Here ... Rachel, I'd like to stay here and watch you for a while; I won't do anything, I'll watch how the computer handles electrical shocks."

"Well, Sonia, everyone has their own tastes, it's your right"

"I would like to ask you something ..."

"Tell me"

"Here I would like to undress her ... may I?"

"Ah, I should have guessed, how sloppy; let's just say the suit she's wearing has no specific function. She doesn't strip because the purpose of this treatment is punitive, not for our pleasure. Ok, you can act however you want; modified humans are at your disposal, remember to let them do the immobilization operations, having said that you can play with the guinea pig as you think, the treatment is automatic. What can I say, good evening, I have a half-naked and excited Swede waiting for me and tonight I feel inspired, mmm ... I could put him through the tickle machine ... one day I'll show it to you, Sonia. See you in the morning. "

Sonia doesn't even see Rachel come out, she's been staring morbidly at the Norwegian for a few minutes.

Now he is alone with her; guards are at your disposal outside the gate.

You want to enjoy those moments slowly.

"I don't even know your name bitch; Rachel is right to feel sorry for you. Your angry look denotes a temper that will not give up. And surely you are strong enough to break steel handcuffs, even if they are faulty, and knock out several armed modified humans; even being dressed like now, I can see that you are thin and strong; but we will fix it immediately, I will start to remove your top ... "

Treatment started less than a day ago, so the girl is still at full capacity.

She has a cheerful face with freckles, blue eyes, and a beautiful color on her cheeks.

Four guards enter and tell Sonia to move away, for safety.

"Just take off the top for now, thanks ..."

The guards, with due precautions, unzip the suit and remove the strap around the waist, lifting the suit above the chest; the girl still has a white t-shirt; it doesn't matter, the pleasure will last. They fasten the belt tightly around the waist.

Now it is the turn of the bicep straps, they lift the suit up to the wrists, leaving the arms uncovered; Since his biceps are now free, he twists heavily; Despite being still totally immobilized, the four guards struggle to reattach the straps this time to bare skin.

The analogous operation on the wrists is carried out, for safety, separately between the right and the left.

Sonia now understands why precautions are never excessive.

"They let us..."

Examine the guinea pig again.

In the suit he couldn't tell how muscular and toned his arms were.

Nothing to do with Monica, but she was getting closer; The peculiarity of Monica was that she was splendid in everything. This was still beautiful, but it was slightly out of proportion to other parts of the body, such as the abdomen, which, although soft and muscular, was not comparable to the mass of the arms. Finding a single fault with Monica was difficult, but not impossible.

The girl, with a very fair complexion, is bathed in sweat, her chest rises and falls rapidly in anticipation of immediate treatment.

A strap connected to several blisters was attached to his mouth, preventing him from speaking; it was probably the means of feeding her, since the treatment lasted at least a week. Electrodes on the wrists.

There are threads coming out of the tank top on the chest; you can see a tape that wraps around the chest, covering the nipples.

Sonia begins to stroke the guinea pig on the face, on the chest, on the abdomen, feeling the firmness of the biceps. You decide to take off the tank top while it's tied up. She pulls it out of her sweatpants, tucks it under her belt with difficulty, exposing her wonderful throbbing breasts. Electrodes were placed on the chest both to control the heartbeat and to induce electrical shocks.

He smells it, he's sweating.

"You have a very pretty little body, you know, bitch?"

He licks her on the navel.

"You're salty ... I like you"

The guinea pig has a rebellious impulse: not only will she have to suffer unspeakably for a week, but now she must also suffer the depravities of that lesbian?

He lets out a mixed grunt of anger and frustration and yanks on the straps.

He looks at Sonia with hatred and defiance.

"I see you still have a lot of strength. Guards! Your pants; take them off completely."

The guards are now six, operations are carried out slowly and carefully, using additional straps.

Operation completed.

Sonia understands why the six guards: the legs have impressive muscle mass.

In the anal and vaginal area there are tubes inserted and strategically fixed in order for the guinea pig to perform physiological functions during treatment.

Other electrodes applied to the ankles.

"Guard, I see that the bed has a mechanism, can I spread your legs wider?"

"Of course"

The guard acts on gears that extend the legs of the guinea pig almost perpendicular to the torso.

The elasticity of the girl is impressive.

Sonia, standing between the guinea pig's legs, her hands resting gently on her bare thighs, stares at her prey. She strokes her legs as they instinctively contract in an attempt to escape and looks into her eyes.

"Are you still thinking of challenging me?"

Sonia says, leaning down to kiss her navel and abdomen in various places.

With chilling slowness he leaves that tempting position to move behind her, always keeping one finger in contact with her body and sliding it in a sensual way.

The guinea pig is furious and tries to say something through the gag in a language unknown to Sonia.

Now Sonia is behind her and, placing her hands on the guinea pig's biceps, she begins to sensually kiss her forehead, cheeks, neck, and ears.

At the same time, he slides his hands over the armpits, the breasts, greedily massaging them and testing their firmness.

The guinea pig complains in protest trying to say something.

Sonia returns to her side and looks at her smiling.

"Hey, what do you have to say? I don't speak your language. You know what? I'm usually more sadistic, less sweet, but ... the fact that I suck you, I'm sorry, makes you instinctively rebellious to my touches and that makes me like it so much ... "

and again runs his hands over the abdomen and breasts.

Suddenly, the computer makes a strange sound similar to an alarm.

The guinea pig's eyes are now filled with terror and they go looking for Sonia for desperate help. From these details, Sonia understands that the treatment is beginning again.

Initially, he emits a cry of rare intensity, but freezes in his throat after a second. The intensity of the torture is such that the guinea pig cannot make a sound.

Sonia watches the animal with interest. The torture remains constant for a few seconds throughout the body, and then alternates with variable intensity, in some areas, to allow a physiological recovery time and not reduce too much sensitivity to pain.

When the legs are stimulated, Sonia can barely visually feel a tic, a permanent contraction in the guinea pig's quadriceps; therefore, it is placed back between the legs and puts the hands on the thighs. The moment the shock begins, you feel the contraction of the muscles touching them much more, despite the position of the legs and the tight straps.

Now the download is going elsewhere.

Driven by an instinct of "compassion", she approaches her mons pubis with her mouth, keeping her hands on her thighs and caressing them.

His tongue slides where it can, between probes and electrodes, stimulating that sensitive part. Cries of protest from the victim.

Now look at the upper body. When hit by the shock, it contracts pecs, biceps, and abs in an unnatural way at the same time. Sonia can see the beauty of his muscles, glistening with the guinea pig's sweat.

For twenty-five minutes he enjoys watching the girl's suffering and admiring her athletic body at the same time.

From time to time he runs his greedy hands over her skin to sadistically caress her, sometimes pinching her, sometimes sensually feeling her.

When the chest is "at rest" the contractions diminish, but immediately the chest begins to rise and fall convulsively again. Between those moments Sonia continues to savor the victim's body by licking and smelling.

Finally, straddling her thigh, while a shock hits her chest, she licks her navel and bites her, finding in that act a pleasure that she has not felt for a long time, precisely since she had seen Monica, on the pole, in the gym.

When the treatment stops, Sonia gathers herself, runs a hand over the girl's abdomen and breasts, noting that her eyes are now expressionless, although they retain that touch of anger and frustration that Sonia likes so much. Clearly, the treatment is starting to work.

"I enjoyed having you my way, bitch. I think I'll visit you again these days."

A kiss on the cheeks.

"Guards, dress her well."

An old friend

It's time for Rachel to say goodbye.

Sonia is a little sorry, she was growing fond, but Rachel reassures her.

"Don't worry, I'll visit you from time to time to have fun; I have my eye on a Cuban boy, a jailer who is not bad at all, all natural ..."

Now Sonia is in charge.

Member 231 is presented to his office as ordered.

He congratulates her, explains how her insertion has been more than satisfactory.

Speaking of the situation on the island, it turns out that George is retiring, but is struggling to find a worthy replacement.

Sonia's mind delves into her memories and someone immediately comes to mind ...

"Member 231 ... here, I'd like to suggest a person's name ..."

Robert, after deep disappointment with Monica, falls into a state of deep depression.

The misfortune of the lake is known to practically everyone. The one with the waterfall a little less.

The companies that contacted you stop looking for you. Parents pressure him by ignoring his feelings.

Feelings for Monica that little by little give way to hatred.

Robert cultivates a deep hatred for whoever rejected him.

In addition, that kick in the genital area, previously not very vigorous and somewhat "useless", now made him almost incapable of having sex. Therefore, being unable to have normal sexual relations for reasons of insecurity, he focuses his sexuality on sadism.

The Internet favors you a lot in this. In any case, he usually pays prostitutes who allow themselves to be tied up to satisfy his instincts. By dominating and binding his victims, he achieves pleasure.

What happened to Sonia is now seen with envy and disgust.

Basically he realizes that the only way for HIM to have a woman is to do it against her will. And since he's not very physically gifted ... the only way, you know what it is, the circle narrows.

He's still an unspoken genius, but with a few complaints from some hookers who aren't very accommodating when it comes to BDSM fantasies, they make his resume not the best.

And he has to find work.

He goes to the umpteenth interview almost with resignation.

The fifty-year-old lady welcomes you to her study.

"Robert, here you are, finally. We need to improve our recruiting division, and while it is true that we were about to lose an element like you ... it was not thanks to ... YOU."

Sonia reveals herself.

Has changed.

Besides having grown up, she also looks more relaxed and happy than the Sonia she had met.

They shake hands.

"Robert, you grew up, but you haven't changed much ..."

Sonia tells her friend all her vicissitudes, from the episodes with Monica, to the recruitment, the group, her job, to how she manages to feel pleasure and satisfaction now.

Robert is incredulous, but decides to accept.

He will be responsible for the Center's computing, sensors and electronics.

The day of the settlement, her amazement at seeing the island is great, Sonia smiles thinking about when she had tried the same things.

All the alarm, control, video surveillance, machinery tests are explained to Robert.

His computer skills, along with his knowledge of mechanics, stimulate various ideas in him, which he will soon put into practice.

George is a patient and methodical teacher.

After a general introduction, Robert visits the "training" area, in particular the pool.

The pool is visibly longer than a regular olimpic pool, deeper and with a three meter high rim, making it impossible for guinea pigs to escape.

Robert watches the procedure in fascination: the guinea pigs in bathing suits approach the pool, with their hands tied behind their backs and their ankles connected with a four-inch long chain (to give a minimal possibility of movement). The electrodes are placed on the chest (for women under a one-piece bathing suit) and tied around the chest. A monitor tracks your pulse. They are hung upside down with a winch, their hands and then their feet are released, causing them to go into the water. Today they are subjected to a long-distance endurance test.

"But how can we be sure that they do their best?"

"Oh, you see, Robert - Sonia intervenes, who is currently on the monitors - it's simple: The latter is subjected to a painful (but basically harmless) pain resistance test; the former is left 'at rest' for a few days ... of course we don't want the same people to suffer, so we usually give the weaker ones a chronometric advantage based on the latest tests ... let's just say it's a lot at our discretion; the important thing is that these stupid beasts they don't realize it and they always push to the maximum "

Robert is surprised by the confidence Sonia has compared to a few years ago; now he is in charge of the genetic division; but it certainly seems to have maintained that coldness that has always characterized it.

The men begin their test that they start separately, so that the chronometric data can be "fixed" without difficulty.

Now it is the turn of the women.

Robert immediately notices the preferences of his colleagues; Among women, Sonia is the only one with a predilection for guinea pigs and seems not to be ashamed of it. Among men, only a certain Paul, a clumsy little man, seems to have equal fun with both sexes. He hears him addressing Sonia saying "tonight I wouldn't mind taking the Cuban and the dancer to my room and spanking them together; ah, for the test I would like to have the Cuban, he tried to rebel when I touched him ... do you understand? "

Sonia nods disinterestedly.

Robert is struck by a swimmer: brown hair, cat-brown eyes, imposing but slender physique.

"Who is it, George?"

"Ah, Gabriela! She is a complete Italian athlete (swimming, running, shot put) who has arrived two weeks ago. We are going to do several physical tests, to see where she does better, although given her beauty she could also be included between the 'entertainment', who knows "

Robert watches as the modified humans position it to carry it into the water with the mechanism. By hanging, he hints at an instinctive move to get up and contract his magnificent abs. Once in the water, upon departure, he starts off with impressive speed and power; his musculature almost matches Monica's, although he remains a step below.

"George ... I think ... I have a request ..."

"Ah, I knew it! It caught your attention right away, right? Well, it is not yet counted among the 'entertainment', but since you are new we will make an exception, I will ask Sonia to let her win, to keep her rested tomorrow at night, and make the special request to Member 231. "

The day goes by smoothly.

The first dinner on the island is also positive for Robert, helped a lot by Sonia, who makes him feel very comfortable.

When it comes to choosing the "victims" for the night, Robert already has a particular request.

"Well George, Member 231, all these guinea pigs are very beautiful and I will certainly appreciate them. But I would like to spend my first night with Gabriela, the Italian athlete, but since it will only be available for tomorrow, today I would like to 'visit 'to each one of you, like this, just to understand your tastes and how' entertainment 'works, always if this is allowed ... and with you too, Member 231, I would be interested to see what you like "

Colleagues gladly accept.

The first one he sees is his tutor, George.

A young and busty blonde (a German prostitute) is tied to her bed half-naked, George brings a cart with ice, food of various kinds, wine near the bed. Obviously he likes to have traditional relationships, with some variations related to food and, obviously, the necessary precautions that require the immobilization of guinea pigs.

Her friend Sonia has a black sprinter in her room. She is naked, tied in an X vertically and slightly raised from the ground. Sonia is applying electrodes all over his body.

"Does it remind you of something, Sonia?"

Silence between the two.

Sonia hints at a smile. Both are united by a mad desire for a certain person. Monica's nostalgia makes them almost melancholic.

Robert decides to leave her there and go elsewhere, to dispel the memory of the old school friend.

Samantha and Julia, two women in their forties, not beautiful, but certainly caring women, charged with feeding and monitoring the health of the guinea pigs, are in the same room with a muscular, naked, firmly tied to some kind of gynecological table. A retractor keeps the mouth open. Thick straps on wrists, biceps, neck, abdomen, thighs and ankles securely immobilize you in bed with your legs spread.

As Samantha gropes the man she slowly turns on, Julia explains to Robert:

"We have fun like this, we arouse him in every possible way, we tease him, we play with him, to keep him on the verge of orgasm. When he is on the verge of despair ... well, it depends on how good he is begging"

With that said, he joins his colleague and patiently begins to work on the victim's body. Julia seems to have more experience, as the man suffered a noticeable erection with her touch.

Samantha looks a bit resentful and slaps him.

"So you prefer her? Damn dog!"

And she bites his ear violently, while Julia continues her work sensually.

Robert goes to the sadistic Paul.

A woman and a man, both black, are tied up facing each other, in their underwear. Obvious signs of spanking in the body of both, more in the woman.

Robert says hello, he has no special sympathy for the man.

The Member 231.

Robert knocks on the door.

"Ahead"

A half-naked man and woman are gagged and immobilized on a strange contraption, with rotating brushes, pens, toothpicks.

"Tickle machine, Robert. I selected the most sensitive items, not the most attractive, as you can see. Look."

The woman presses a button. The brushes and feathers begin to dance on the most sensitive parts of the two poor people; armpits, hips, feet, neck are the most stressed areas.

The woman, especially, writhes like a fury, screams convulsively.

Robert is fascinated by all this.

However, he retires to his room. His preference for Gabriela the next day is actually an excuse to retreat to his room and turn on his old PC: nostalgia captures him, the photos of his beloved Monica, now a young and promising athlete, are meticulously and obsessively preserved by him ; from the most banal photographic poses to the still images captured during his performances.

He cannot forget her.

You're about to find another video or article when you hear a knock on your door.

"Sonia, come, come in"

"Hi Robert, how are you?"

"Well look, I'll never thank you enough for making me go this far. I'll never be able to pay you back."

"Well, you should know that it is a pleasure for me to have a person here that I have known since high school."

They talk like two old friends, they talk about this and that, Sonia talks about her sadistic work like nothing.

At one point Sonia presses:

"You keep thinking ... about her. Right?"

In response, Robert shows Sonia the photos on his PC. Sonia is amazed to see the number of photos of the victim of her dreams, divided into folders and subfolders: videos, interviews, articles, photos, sports performances.

Just thinking about what he could do to her on the island makes her fly with her imagination like never before. A photo in which Monica is struggling with the pole vault captures her attention: the athlete has just left the pole, her face concentrated in the effort, the slender muscles tense and sinuous at the same time, the frantic upper part rises. Discover the abdomen and all the sculpted abdominal muscles.

Sonia flies and dreams of Monica on the island as a guinea pig, but a thought seizes her:

"Robert ... you ... love her right? I mean in a traditional way, you would never hurt her, you would want her to yourself, if she were a guinea pig here you would like to free her to show her your love ... truth? "

"Sonia ... you don't know how much I've changed. Growing up and colliding with reality, with your physical appearance, you come to understand that you can never have a creature like that, how could she fall in love with me? Look, my desire for her hasn't changed, in fact, stronger than before, but there is a difference.

You may not know that the kick he gave me that day caused me quite a few sexual problems; I'm not at all helpless, but I struggle to have ... here you know what; instead, the idea of having a woman in my power excites me a lot. Monica then ... let's not talk about it.

I want to humiliate her, like she did to me. I want him to suffer. I want him to regret having humiliated me. I want to tear her out of the world she knows and have her here to torture her slowly, without damaging her too much. I want her to become a slave, an object in my hands. But she must suffer, rebel, I want to hear her scream with rage "

Robert's eyes light up and meet Sonia's.

The magic of the situation, the meeting between the two, the feelings revealed break down the barriers between the two. Almost ecstatic, the two embrace, then, holding hands and looking at Monica's photo, they begin to caress each other.

Now they are accomplices.

They are not attracted to each other. But his wish goes in the same direction.

"Robert, if you knew how many times I've talked to member 231 ... the fact is, she's famous you know? Too many eyes on her. Too many people on her trail. It would take a miracle, I don't know, to get her arrested, or ... bah. The point is, I don't want to fool myself. And we have something to comfort us here anyway, don't you think? "

Robert nods, not very convinced.

Pleasant pastime

Robert is in his room, watching the news on television.

How long does it take? They should be here for a few minutes - he thinks.

They knock on the door.

"Ah, finally"

The modified humans enter the room with a cart.

Gabriela is traditionally X-tied, blindfolded and with a retractor in her mouth.

As Robert ordered, she is dressed in a white panties and tank top.

They are left alone.

As the guinea pig begins to tug on the leashes, wondering why the endless wait, Robert, with sadistic patience, turns around and takes a close look at his prey.

It is the first time you have found your dreams come true.

The guinea pig is a magnificent specimen. Now that she's tied up, every inch of her fabulous body can be observed up close.

With a finger and gently, Robert begins to tease and pinch her here and there; it's nice to see her shake, her muscles get more prominent; You can test their consistency by pinching and nibbling on the pectoral and bicep area.

Butt is an anthem to perfection, sinuous and toned.

Robert plays with the elastic of the panties testing the firmness of the buttocks.

He had already tied up some prostitutes, but they all consented anyway; and in any case they allowed themselves to be tied in a very false way.

Now everything was different.

Besides, he hadn't seen such a body yet; Sure, Monica's body was unattainable, but this "substitute" was nevertheless remarkable. Furthermore, he never had time to examine Monica's body closely, except on those brief occasions when she would hit him.

Now Gabriela was there, tied up and at her mercy. I wanted to enjoy that moment.

Clack ... clack ... Robert had decided to put more stress on her, to reduce her freedom of movement; Arms and legs well stretched, although not to the limit.

Rass ... with scissors cut the straps of the tank top, at the top.

A magnificent chest, with exposed ribs (given the position), but with nice and firm breasts.

The retractor is attached to a bar at the top to hold it edge up.

So much strength and power in his hands.

With a toothpick he pricks her thighs, abdomen, armpits.

His involuntary reflexes are what satisfies him the most.

Over time, she discovered that she loved traditional sex less and less. The victim's vain attempts at rebellion excite him violently.

Out with the panties.

Robert patiently moves to her genital area and begins, with tweezers, annoyingly pulling the hair ... tac; here is a disappearing pubic hair, resulting in the moaning of the victim.

He likes to alternate rapid and decisive outbursts with prolonged and painful ones for the victim, who begins to sweat.

Sweat makes Gabriela's body shine in a visually pleasing way.

Robert smells it and licks it all over the place, then goes back to the painful waxing.

Tonight, Robert understands that all his past sufferings will be partially justified by the satisfactions he will derive from that moment. Gabriela is the first victim of the humiliation and physical pain that the sadistic and patient Robert can cause.

Using the unfortunate as a guinea pig, Robert experiments with electrostimulation on her, reaching limits that he would never have thought of reaching in a human.

He feels like a God, having full control over the beautiful athlete.

The pleasure obtained after two hours of torture alternated with small games is very satisfying for Robert, who falls asleep for several hours.

Upon awakening, you see your guinea pig exhausted from the position in which she was tied up all night, but still responds to your touch.

Release the chain attached to the retractor so I can see your face. He kisses her enthusiastically, with a movement of revulsion from the victim, and then slaps her angrily, venting all his frustration at his disappointment with Monica.

If only he were here in poor Gabriela's place ... a hint of nostalgia takes hold of the boy.

In the months that followed, Robert worked hard to keep all the surveillance systems and all the electrical and mechanical devices used for both the experiments and the "sessions" efficient. Thanks to his imagination and his genius, he is able to develop a much safer and more efficient system than his now old predecessor.

The harmony with Sonia and the common passion, reinforced by their very similar tastes, allows them to achieve excellent results in research, far beyond the forecasts of Member 231.

They are often found after dinner to play with guinea pigs, torturing, raping and even humiliating them.

Other nights, however, they find themselves nostalgically admiring the photos of their beloved Monica G.

A torture that they are unable to perform, despite the innumerable diversions that the situation offers.

Christmas of the year 2018 is approaching, when Member 231, on Christmas Eve, calls them both for a meeting.

"Sit down dear ones. You have no idea how far we've come, thanks mostly to you, in the last few months. Especially on the new prototypes of modified humans and the ability to telepathically control them via other modified humans. It was something that nobody would have thought. Not even I tried to imagine. Not to mention the modernized structures thanks to the genius of our Robert "

Robert and Sonia look at each other, a little flushed, but aware that the compliments are deserved.

"There is something, however, that makes them a little sad, everyone knows it, even if they never talk about it"

The two do not know how to respond to the woman.

"Well, I don't normally take work personally for this kind of thing, but I made an exception for them as they joined in and gave so much to the group."

They look a bit surprised, wondering the meaning of the woman's words.

"Well ... to be honest I don't know if I could have done it, if the events hadn't helped me ... among other things, it's funny that tomorrow is Christmas; well, I can't wait for tomorrow to surprise you with a gift ... "

Sonia interrupts ...

"And that cut, member 231?"

Christmas 2018 - the most beautiful Christmas

Monica G., aka Fantastic Girl, wakes up lying on the floor of a strange, almost futuristic cell; It seems to him that he is in a science fiction film, the white walls, the dim light, a glass through which nothing is seen.

She gets up a little stunned. The moment he realizes that he has his gray disguise but no longer the mask, he remembers everything: the night, the fight, his victory, the dart ... and then again the police, the strangers who break in. , then nothing.

Where is? She is trapped in a cell, but where?

Not knowing what to do, he begins to kick and push against the glass, but with no other effect than hurting his shoulder; and say that, thanks to his strength, he had broken down several doors in this way, and not in a subtle way.

A light on the other side of the glass.

A dozen men in blue overalls enter the room on the other side of the glass, the same kind of uniform you saw earlier. They are all armed, two carry a car with some strange gadgets, Monica can only recognize some strange straps that apparently serve to immobilize.

Finally, a woman ... wait, he recognizes her, she's the same one from the police station from Sonia's time, and the same one who asked her the fateful question "Are you Fantastic Girl?"

"What's going on here? Where are the police? Who are you, what do you want from me? I haven't killed anyone, not even stolen, this is illegal ..."

"But how many words, my dear Monica, or Fantastic Girl what you want. Listen, I'll tell you everything later and very calmly ... uh, uh, you won't believe me, but we have a lot of time available ..."

"Time? I don't have time for anyone, now I want to make a phone call, I have the right ..."

"Ssshhhh, you see, my dear gymnast - heroine, the first thing to understand is that from now on you will have no rights, like it or not. Now please start taking off that stupid disguise ..."

"Listen to me well, you fucking whore, I don't know who you are, but I'm well known, they'll look for me, I don't take orders from anyone ..."

"Eeeehhh, I already knew that this would end like this, gentlemen, activate the 'heating' ..."

A man in a blue suit flips a switch.

The lights go out, Monica can no longer see anything outside the glass, while the captive is clearly visible from the outside.

Within seconds, the air becomes heavier, warmer, and unbreathable.

Monica begins to wonder how this could happen, where the hell is she. The heat becomes unbearable, the humidity is very high.

Monica is very physically prepared, but after a few minutes she begins to have breathing problems. But he doesn't want to satisfy the woman.

Suddenly, the cell is divided into two parts by metal bars.

The area you are in remains the same; in the other area, Monica sees a kind of nozzle coming out of the ceiling. At a certain point, water starts to come out of the nozzle.

Monica begins to understand.

With all her might she tries to bend the bars to somehow pass, but in addition to being stunned by the narcotic, she is also exhausted from the sudden heat.

"You see, my dear gymnastic friend, you should have realized by now that if you want to get to the other side, you have to take off that stupid costume, you see the bars will still be there until you take it off. Oh, and you know we can shoot you a tranquilizer dart anytime and do what we want, if you prove stupidly stupid. Hey come on, now the temperature is above forty degrees, the water is quite cold, don't you want to cool off?"

Monica's survival instincts prevail over pride.

Not without some difficulties, given the humidity, exhaustion and sweat, he manages to completely undress and throw his "stupid disguise" on the floor.

Nothing happens.

"Hey, I got naked, what else do you want me to do? Damn it!" Monica screams with a hint of frustration in her voice.

After a sadistic wait, the woman responds.

"Put the stupid disguise in this slot"

A container comes out from under the glass. Monica puts on the costume.

Member 231 sniffs the sweat from the guinea pig in costume.

In response, a man flips a switch, the bars are raised, Monica throws herself into the shower and lets the water slide all over her body, ignoring the prying eyes of her captors.

The lights come back on.

The woman applauds.

"Well done, do you see that you are not as stupid as your appearance may suggest?"

The woman begins to see her prey in a different light; thinks to herself.

"Damn, what a physique. Now I understand Robert and Sonia's obsession with that woman. I don't think I've ever seen such a well-made guinea pig among all the athletes I've experimented with in over twenty years, even though I like men. "Such a woman can turn anyone into a lesbian. Almost almost ... I could have her immobilized right away, but let's see how the fight comes on; I haven't done it for years, but I'll have you believe you can escape ..." although modified humans complain if one of their companions is injured "

"Now my beautiful Monica, my men will enter and immobilize you, in the meantime I have other things to do, please, behave if you do not want to be ... punished; gentlemen, it is all yours, I LEAVE THE KEYS TO THE BUILDING IN THE HANDS OF THE CAPTAIN Bring her to the office pretty tied up in fifteen minutes. "

Member 231 lets in the other ten modified humans, armed only with batons, chains, and handcuffs, one in a red suit, different from the others.

Monica is naked, wet, and exhausted from the heat, but her fighting habit has taught her to evaluate every situation.

Count ten, of which the red one must necessarily be the captain. They do not appear to carry weapons other than truncheons. And from what she understands, they want her alive. That is a huge advantage for someone like her. Faced with the absurd situation, he decides to make at least one desperate attempt.

Two of them come up behind her with handcuffs and ties, two more in front of her; the others wait with truncheons ready to intervene.

When they take her arms from behind, she holds them tightly and throws them against the two in front, throwing them on the ground;

the two grabbed by her are neutralized by violently hitting both heads against each other.

Now five men armed with batons are approaching from all sides at the same time. With a powerful, quick instinctual leap, he launches himself at one, disarms it, and earns himself a truncheon. The others pounce on her and two manage to violently hit her knees, causing her to fall. The other two take advantage and hit her again in the abdomen, but she, almost as if she had not noticed the blows, surrounds them with a somersault.

Member 231 watches the scene from a hidden camera. He had sent ten combat-trained modified humans armed with batons. He fought them with impressive ease. His jumps and kicks were incredible. Three of them remained. Monica had dropped the baton, her arms even more deadly. With his marble legs he squeezed one victim until he passed out, while with both hands he held the rest to the ground. He addresses the only survivor, the "captain".

From what he could see, probably less than half were still alive. A deadly weapon, a fierce fighter.

The poor man hands her the keys trembling, then she hits him with her fist as if it were made of paper.

"Exceptional. Take another twenty in ..."

Member 231 leaves the monitor to go down.

The group of modified humans, in addition to being twenty, have a network that facilitates their work.

After capturing her with the net like an animal, they manage to handcuff her to her back and ankles and put a kind of collar on her.

They take it off the net.

"Look up"

Monica stands in front of member 231, approximately eight inches taller than her.

Up close he can appreciate her body, still panting from the fierce fight that is still going on.

A modified human keeps her tied, two others hold her arms, already handcuffed, with two chains at the ankles, also tied.

Naked and wet.

What impresses is the irrepressible femininity, beauty combined with strength, a specimen more unique than rare.

Those throbbing breasts were so attractive.

"You know honey, I'm definitely straight, I'm crazy about men. But you ... here's something unique, sculpted abs ... what arms and shoulders ... and your legs, what perfection ... you're sweaty. .. hot "

The dark-haired athlete dates back to when she was tied up and tortured by Sonia.

Now he was in a much worse situation, and not just because he didn't see a way out.

Tied up Naked That woman's eyes on her.

His heart begins to beat strongly in his chest when the woman begins to caress his breasts, abdomen, buttocks.

In a last desperate effort he manages to find the strength to kick with both feet tied to the woman's face, now on the ground with a bleeding lip.

"Damn my stupidity ... never go near a guinea pig in person. Put her to bed, use double leashes!"

The modified humans, despite the numerical superiority, the handcuffs, leashes and chains already attached to Monica, struggle long before they tie her completely to the cot, blindfold her and gag her with a retractor.

"Now it's safe, ma'am"

"Good. Stay away"

He approaches the bed with the woman tied up like a salami.

The number of straps somewhat limits the percentage of bare skin that can be admired, but it's a pretty sight, in any case, and at that point it's best to be safe.

"You see, bitch, no one has ever kicked me. Now, I'm a fair woman and I won't do anything to you, because I have to leave you intact for ... two people you know well, you are a prize to them, you know?" And I'm holding back The time will come, coldly, when I will make you pay. As I already told you, time is not lacking at all "

With that said, he takes her right nipple and squeezes it hard.

Monica writhes more with humiliation than pain.

"I like the sound of a naked body on the straps. Take it to the office. Tie it to the 'dessert' cart, I'll fix it myself."

Monica doesn't see anything because of the blindfold, she just feels that she is being taken elsewhere.

A door closes. The expert hands of several people quickly apply new straps to you before removing the old ones. With experience and manic patience, she is immobilized to stand.

Cold water all over the body.

Soap.

The hands of several people, but rush, feel no desire. It feels like an object.

They rinse him off.

With the same procedure now they immobilize her in a car, always held.

It stretches until it checks that there is no possibility of movement.

As if that were not enough, they apply straps above and below the knees, on the thighs both in the middle and near the groin, on the waist, on the abdomen, above and below the breasts, on the neck, above and below the elbows. In the mouth another retractor with a rising rod, the only opening through which it can breathe, since the nose is closed with clips. In the eyes a rim that, in addition to showing nothing, does not allow him to move his head an inch.

It is inexorably immobile.

If they had wanted to kill her, they would have. What will happen to her? What two people was she talking about?

His thoughts are interrupted by the sensation of a kind of foam being sprayed on his body.

You pull a switch and feel the temperature drop.

We stay with Robert and Sonia in the office.

"And that cut, member 231?"

The lady smiles and reveals a cut on her lip.

"You don't read the newspapers, do you? Better this way, everything will be more beautiful. Ah, the cut I have? Well, don't worry, nothing serious, whoever did it will have time to regret it, given what awaits here. Now agree to be my guests for dinner tonight. By the way, I took the liberty of inhibiting the telematics systems in your rooms, so you won't be able to follow the news ... but only for tonight. "

"We gladly accept, Member 231. See you tonight"

Member 231 generally eats alone or with everyone else, rarely dining with other people.

Robert and Sonia go to their boss's room.

"Welcome, come early. I understand you, you know? Have a seat."

Three chairs, nothing in between.

"But what...?"

"Waiters, please"

Two modified humans enter with a cart.

Robert recognizes the cart: the victims are completely immobilized, and their bodies are doused with food to brighten up dinners in an unusual way. This time the body was completely covered. A refrigerator kept the temperature low to store the cream. A masterpiece, this time they were busy. Cream and meringue all over the body. The large breasts were covered in cream with cherries on the nipples. The face covered with a hollow melon and a ham around it.

At the top a breathing tube. A coconut in the middle in the groin area, strategic. And then cream. Cream and meringue.

The low temperature made the guinea pig shudder, but movement was nearly impossible due to the countless straps that contained it.

She was completely covered, but they could already guess that the woman's physique was spectacular: tall, sharp, but with considerable muscle mass, a toned and full chest; and they hadn't seen the best yet.

The waiter brings melted chocolate.

"Serve yourself"

Sonia pours hot chocolate on his abdomen. The victim gasps, followed by a "nnnggghhhhh!" suffocated.

Diners begin to savor the delicacy from the abdomen.

"Nice this arrangement, we should do it a little more often"

Robert jokes, dipping his silver fork into the meringue.

After a couple of minutes, the abdomen is quite bare. Diners can appreciate the muscular, sculpted abs, but still sinuous and smooth. The guinea pig is dark-skinned, but western.

Robert likes to tease her with the tip of his fork, causing small imperceptible contractions of the abs.

Member 231 deactivates the refrigerant.

"Time to try it, don't you think?"

Sonia pours hot chocolate over her now uncovered abdomen. The guinea pig lets out a cry and squirms more. Despite the straps, his pulls make the icing fall on the right nipple, on Sonia's side.

"But look, it looks like our little friend is rebelling. Look, Robert, she ruined the decor."

Robert intervenes.

"Well, in the meantime, let's tape the straps"

Monica, through the blanket of food, manages to hear the voices. Those familiar voices ... no ... it can't be. It must be a nightmare ...

"Where is the button, Sonia? Ah, there it is, how stupid"

Hearing that name is like a blow to the heart for Monica who, in a panic, begins to squirm with all the strength of which she is capable.

The other frosting falls off, some of the meringue around the arms gives way, the straps seem to loosen.

Robert presses a button.

The leashes are tightened until the guinea pig calms down again, which is now breathing more pronouncedly.

The efforts and sweat have melted part of the decoration, now you can see the shoulders, armpits, biceps, thighs, in addition to the abdomen already exposed.

Now the two of them can see more details of the victim's body, appreciate the muscle definition and the firmness of the flesh. They do not remember ever seeing a guinea pig like that.

"That cream looks appetizing"

That puts pressure on Sonia and she immediately begins to lick her breasts greedily, followed by Robert.

More than eating the excellent cream, its purpose is to discover fantastic, abundant, firm, round breasts, perfectly linked to the pectorals, which culminate in large, dark and fleshy nipples.

After unfastening the straps above and below the breasts, they observe how the contractions of the pectorals cause the breasts to move in a vital and rebellious way.

Sweat begins to form in the armpits.

The two anxiously pass their fingers and tongue.

"I want to see her squirm ... I have an idea"

Robert puts his hand on the snorkel and closes it.

After a minute, the guinea pig begins to move like a fury. Sonia, meanwhile, bites down on the nipple in a nasty way causing the guinea pig to jump.

Robert opens the respirator.

The breast begins to rise and fall frantically, Robert takes the opportunity to lick it greedily.

Repeat the game three or four times observing that the cream is already almost completely dissolved.

Member 231 watches them with pleasure; he wonders if they already suspect something. At this point he also participates by nibbling the guinea pig's inner thigh and watching its muscles contract. It had never happened to him that he wanted a woman ... until now.

After twenty minutes of cruel games, the body is completely naked, except for the straps. And the face covered.

Robert and Sonia stop for a moment to admire it.

The definition, the sinuosity of the whole is incredible. Legs that seem to have marble buttocks on them.

"I must say that this time we have reached a limit. I don't think there can be a more beautiful body than this. Whose face will that be. Only one person can match that, and you know who I mean, Robert ..."

The two look at each other.

The shadow of doubt crosses their faces.

Member 231 gets it.

"Guys, I think you want to enjoy this moment alone, but first ... here, yesterday's newspaper. I suggest you read the title on the second page ... then you can take that stupid melon away."

He walks away and leaves the room.

They are both realizing that maybe ...

Their hearts beat a thousand.

Sonia reads aloud:

"SENSATIONAL: Fantastic Girl turns out to be the promise of world athletics Monica G., considered by all almost an alien for her athletic gifts, not least for her beauty. But the day of capture she manages to escape somehow. Perhaps with the help of accomplices. The fact is that she neutralized two guards and fled. No one finds her, she did not appear for training. The police have already issued the border alert. The truth is that, before she was a heroine loved by all, after killing two officers is guilty of murder ... "

Monica hears Sonia's words and begins to cry desperately. Now everything is clear. She is naked, immobilized and at the mercy of two crazy psychopaths. With the force of desperation, crying, she pulls the straps unnaturally, managing to break the ones that surround her right elbow.

Robert presses the "emergency" button and additional straps immediately pop out of the mechanism, irretrievably immobilizing the guinea pig; now you can see her tears of despair under the melon.

Robert and Sonia approach the guinea pig, slowly wiping the little food left on the body with napkins, remaining sadistically on all areas sensitive to touch, while she writhes in despair.

When he no longer has the strength to cry, they take care of the melon and the tube, uncovering his face and eyes.

Monica already got it, but seeing them in the face is like a stab. How could that happen? She will never forgive her quirk of being a superhero

Sonia and Robert watch her ecstatically. A dream come true.

Monica, in his presence, defenseless, but with all her might. Your physical strength won't do you any good. Now it belongs to them.

As possessed they begin to kiss her on the face, on the ears, caress her with renewed desire; while Robert takes care of the face, the breasts, Sonia glides, with nervous tongue and fingers, over the abdomen, thighs, buttocks, genitals.

Monica begins to scream in panic and frustration, the straps tight in "emergency" mode prevent her from moving, she has been sweating for several minutes and not from physical effort.

"Let me go! Damn, what do you want from me? You worm, we've studied together for years ... no ... no ... stop ... don't try, you know ... aaaaahhhhhhhh!"

Robert, having let her vent, bites her right nipple in annoyance, pulling up, painfully for the poor guinea pig, while with his hand he squeezes the left one.

Sonia takes care of the lower part, not without a hint of malice, aware of the "bath" that Monica had forced her to do. He bites, pinches, explores with his tongue.

Monica, crying, breathes heavily and tries to think of a possible way out.

She sees his magnificent chest glistening with sweat, feels the desire of his tormentors, their tongues and their fingers sliding over her.

She begins to marvel at herself when a strange sensation takes over her; futile efforts to free themselves are marked by guttural, almost animal sounds. The straps in emergency mode, although they are safer, allow a minimum of freedom of movement, being more elastic; In this way Mónica has the opportunity to force them, highlighting her imposing muscles, with great thanks to Robert and Sonia. She knows she doesn't stand a chance, but she keeps pulling, like an animal, almost ... almost like she likes those two to see her in that state. No, it is not possible.

After countless jerks accompanied by growls, Sonia notices an unmistakable sign of the guinea pig's arousal.

"Hey Robert, come see this little bitch ..."

Robert puts a finger in the offensive area.

"But look, who would have thought that"

They smile at the immobilized victim, who tries to hide the redness on his cheeks.

Monica, desperately trying to dismiss the thought, begins to scream.

"Help ... Hey, can anyone hear me? You two have very strange ideas, damn it, if I ever break free I won't let you get up again like I did the last few times"

Member 231 bursts into the room with ten modified humans.

"Guys please ... we have plenty of time for that. Now let the modified humans take her to her cell, and let me exchange a few words with her ... after all, you are my guest, you filthy bitch."

Run a finger across her abdomen to reach her nipple and squeeze.

Monica squirms and keeps a proud, defiant look at the woman.

"You and I need to have a conversation about who is in charge here and who should NOT be allowed to look at me that way."

He says it severe but controlled.

The modified humans go with the car.

FIFTH PART
MONICA'S BODY - FANTASTIC GIRL

Introducing the new guinea pig

There is a lot of excitement on the island. Everyone knows that there is a new acquisition. It is a fairly common occurrence, but this time it seems that things are different. Partly because everyone knows who Monica G. is, her athletic prowess, the way she was caught, as a superhero; After the news of the capture, everyone went to see photos of the woman on the Internet, taken from sporting goods or from videos in which she participated in pole vaulting. Above all, everyone wonders why she was not included among the guinea pigs like everyone else. This causes slight discontent on the island, so member 231 summons Robert and Sonia to his office.

The two of them are still in shock from capturing their object of desire.

Sonia takes the floor.

"This ... member 231, we really don't know what to say ... saying thank you is little"

Tears of joy in her anguished eyes, almost incredulous at the grace received.

Robert ecstatic, unable to speak.

Now they can take revenge on whoever humiliated them in the past and, at the same time, have it as and when they want.

The fantasies of the two run wild, renewed by what they have always wanted, possible torture, tests of strength, even keeping her naked and tied in the room to humiliate her.

Member 231 stops the ravings of the two.

"Guys, first of all, you have nothing to thank me for. Having a specimen like Monica here was something we had been waiting for a long time. An opportunity like this came up with her 'foolishness' to become a superhero with what He made it easy for us. The reason you don't have to thank me for anything ... is that EVERYONE on the island will be able to appreciate ... your qualities, plus there are many tests - experiments that require a female with these characteristics "

The two of them had never considered it from this point of view and a touch of anger - jealousy catches them off guard.

Sonia, a little scared, intervenes.

"But ... well ... with all due respect, but using a female ... uh ... guinea pig with this potential for certain tests seems like a waste ..."

"Oh, but you mean the damage it could take ... you know what? You've practically finished the 'regenerative machine'; well, consider it an incentive to speed up your preparations; and, come on, you'll still have it. Robert, you make up that expensive. There are six of us, more than once a week you can 'play' with her, maybe even with your colleague ".

Robert and Sonia feel a bit chilled by their initial overwhelming enthusiasm, but they realize the situation they are in.

"Let's put it like this, you have two days to complete the machine, so ... well then Monica will have to go through the hands of our Paul, lover of the whip; and even through my hands, since she and I have unfinished business."

Monica spends the night in her cell. If it weren't for physical fatigue, I wouldn't be able to sleep; too many questions in his head about where he is, what awaits him in the future. What is the purpose of these people? What will they do to her? Survive to? Both the humiliation and the physical pain scare her. On the physical level, he has never had a problem with enduring pain and fatigue. But what was that feeling of abandonment and relief that had little filled her when she was naked and tied in the hands of those two?

A knock on the mattress wakes him up, she is wearing a light suit.

"Wake up dear, my wayward guinea pig."

Monica realizes that this is not the time to rebel and doesn't say anything disrespectful to member 231.

"Standing".

She obeys.

Member 231 normally should, at this point, order the modified humans to come in, immobilize her hands and feet, then take her to the gym, exercise her, keep her in shape; As the most important thing these days is to assess its potential and for what purpose it could be used.

The normal procedure foresees that, after a morning of work in the gym and the pool, the guinea pig is fed, allowed to rest for a couple of hours and then asked to perform a specific training that can be running, electrostimulation, swimming or specific improvements. Then a final shower, dinner and, for the most pleasant specimens, an evening with one of the members of the island to "brighten up" their stay. Obviously, all guinea pig training sessions are supervised by at least five modified humans; Guinea pigs are always immobilized or placed in places where they cannot do harm (such as the high-edge pool, the fenced-in island path, and the gym with bars).

Member 231, however, instead of going through the normal procedure, lets himself be tempted, he doesn't have the patience to wait for his evening.

"Listen, bitch, I don't want my armed soldiers to pin you down, hurt you, or possibly punish you; you should know that we can stun you with stun guns at any time to get your obedience, one way or another; so I hope you are enough smart enough to obey me "

Silence.

"Well, start jogging on the spot."

Monica, a bit surprised by the request, despite being upset at the pride of being called a "bitch", begins to jog.

His trot on the floor of the room is light and without difficulty.

"Well, raise your knees a little higher"

It does.

After five minutes of light jogging, Monica doesn't feel the slightest sign of fatigue.

"Lift them higher"

Monica looks like a spring, she doesn't have the slightest difficulty. It is impressive how it combines power with grace and elasticity.

Your legs are one with your body in motion.

A perfect whole.

"Stop, breathe a little"

Monica takes the opportunity to catch her breath (even if she didn't need it).

Member 231 doesn't notice a drop of sweat on the guinea pig's face.

"Push-ups, Monica; start push-ups; feet together and body straight; don't stop until I tell you"

Begins.

Perfect.

An impressive facility.

After another five minutes, it shows no signs of abating.

Member 231 must go to the bathroom.

"The captain will check that you are still doing push-ups; I'll be right back; ah, please don't stop and don't slow down, otherwise ... well, we'll find something painful to do right away, bitch."

As the woman walks away, Monica continues with the exercise. Now he somewhat regrets having answered the woman wrong the day before. But he knows that he acted on his instincts and his pride remains intact.

Member 231 comes back from the bathroom and watches the guinea pig. His movement is always regular and smooth, but breathing begins to be difficult.

After fifteen minutes, calculating one pushup per second, you will have done almost nine hundred pushups.

He had seen male guinea pigs numbering three thousand; in any case, when they reached a thousand, their pace dropped dramatically. Monica ... well, just a little gasp.

"With you I want the surveillance to be doubled ... or better, tripled; Captain, let another ten come; there must be fifteen, of which five are armed. Damn it ... I want to see you sweating, I'm impatient. You, get up a little bit the temperature "

Done.

Monica begins to feel tired, sweat forms both from exhaustion and from the heat in the room.

At some point, inevitably, it begins to slow down.

Member 231 is satisfied with the result obtained.

"Well, congratulations; stand up"

Monica, breathing heavily, gets up.

For her it was a show of training, but nothing particularly demanding; only the rise in temperature bothered him.

This is the moment you've been waiting for.

"Take off your clothes".

Reluctantly, he does. Out with the top of the suit.

"Completely; I want you completely naked"

Done.

"Legs apart and hands above the head."

This vision has never been seen by her before. Yet in all these years he had seen many athletes, several blacks; sweat makes their beautiful shapes shine.

From inside the cell, Mónica does what is ordered to avoid immediate retaliation, while maintaining a proud look that witnesses her not submissive temperament.

At a signal from the woman, ten modified humans enter the cell, immobilizing her with double straps (as ordered by the woman) to a bar with hooks that has emerged from the ceiling of the cell, the other five at a safe distance with stun weapons pointed.

By the time her wrists are pinned to the ceiling, Monica still has her legs free and knows she could knock out at least five or six of them; but how to deal with others and especially with armed men? So it also allows your ankles to be tied to the ground. She is now X-tied standing up.

"Pull it up a bit."

The captain operates the bar with a remote control by bringing it closer to the ceiling. When Monica's feet are four inches off the ground and her movements are limited to a certain rocking, the mechanism stops.

Member 231 is in awe.

He slowly approaches Monica in chains and sniffs her.

Your sweat is pleasant to the smell. The breasts, after exertion, have a beautiful pink color; the chest rises and falls showing all the animal femininity of the woman.

Tongue in the armpits. Monica, who had tried to remain motionless so as not to satisfy the woman, jerks uncontrollably and tugs on the straps, much to the appreciation of member 231.

"Mmmm, is it possible that you're ticklish? We'll see, we'll see, maybe another day. Now leave us alone."

The modified humans retreat. Monica wonders what the woman wants from her. He knows he shouldn't have hurt her lip, now covered with a bandage. He makes an instinctive gesture and begins to tug on the straps, which, however, being partly elastic, absorb his effort unharmed and without yielding. Then, he stubbornly renews his effort by bending his arms and legs just enough for more leverage.

"Hey you guys, come back here for a moment! Quick"

Mod humans are back with a great run.

"I want you to add more straps; you better be ultra safe, even if you could never break them anyway, bitch."

Monica is upset, but maintains her demeanor and shows no rejection. Indeed, it would have been impossible to break free, but the woman is very afraid of him, after the previous kick.

Now it's even tighter than before, the extra straps leave you with very little movement.

"Now you can go"

Now they are alone.

Member 231 stares at Monica for five minutes and remains motionless. Monica says nothing and does not reveal emotions.

"Well, you have a good temper, dog."

Monica has a proud gaze and avoids the woman's gaze.

Breathing is calmer now.

"You don't talk. What should you say on the other hand? Bitches don't talk. You could at least apologize for my cut on your lips, didn't they teach you politeness?"

Silence.

At the touch of the woman on the muscular abdomen, Monica jumps.

"Ah, but there you are. Listen, cheeky, in a few days I'll have you all night. I don't know where you come from, how can you be so beautiful and strong at the same time? Sometimes I have thought that there can be no one like this in this planet. Oh, but don't worry. I'll make you suffer. Physically. And then you'll beg me to forgive you. "

Nibble the abdomen around the navel, lick the breasts and nipples. It seems like a dream. He bites down on her left nipple and Monica jerks, more with pride than pain, and turns her head to the side.

"You will look down and beg me to kiss you, saying that I am your only Goddess on Earth."

He bites down on her nipple hard, Monica suppresses a cry, but a "nnnggghhhhh!" it escapes him.

"For today it is fine, but it does not end here ... we will meet again soon; you know, I have command on this island forgotten by the world."

Monica, at the word "island", has a moment of panic. Your chances of escape are practically nil if you are on an island.

For now she is proud that she has not succumbed to the woman.

The modified humans return to their daily routine and the day goes by smoothly.

Sonia and Robert are working assiduously on the regenerative machine.

In practice, it is a giant egg where anyone who sits inside for five minutes can heal from all kinds of wounds, illnesses and injuries. It can't do anything against normal aging, but wearing it every day can greatly extend your life, in theory.

After several attempts with guinea pigs after having them subjected to minor cuts, burns, scrapes, Sonia and Robert went further, subjecting the guinea pigs to severe trauma, sprains, partial mutilations, and then cured them with surprising results. They are now completing tests to improve the reliability and efficiency of the machine.

Robert tests it on himself. Even if he is not injured or sick, he uses it for two minutes. Once outside, it feels like you've just woken up from a days and days sleep, brand new, your posture more upright, your body more toned. She wonders what effect it might have ... on her. Sonia also asks him.

Special meeting.

Meeting room with Sonia, Robert, Julia, Samantha and Paul.

Member 231 enters, the others stand up as a sign of respect.

"Good morning dear colleagues. Today I present to you the long-awaited Monica. There is a lot of curiosity on the part of all, men and women. Among us I confess that when I see her without clothes my heterosexuality falters a lot. Hey, look at this recording: after her capture I saw her and was struck by her physique as well as her face, so I put her gymnastics skills to the test - she struggles giving her a false hope of escape. I can only tell you that she was unarmed. (besides being naked, I couldn't help but undress her) against ten modified humans armed with chains and batons ... well, look ":

The film of the fight proceeds from the initial moments in which she is seen surrounded, at the moment of her attack, then to the blows she receives, she who stands up as if nothing, her momentary victory. After the scene, the video continues with the entry of the other twenty who catch her, not without difficulty, thanks to the network, as well as the obvious numerical superiority. Member 231's fight scene is accompanied by an "Oohhh" of general amazement. Then she was tied to the cot with straps. At the end of the video, some still images highlight some almost unnatural acrobatic movements, as well as his magnificent forms.

Julia and Samantha, notoriously straight, look at each other concerned.

"Member 231, you're right; I don't know my colleague Samantha, but seeing a specimen like that I can switch sides quite easily; hey, look when they hit her, she has a crazy movement; animal but nice; powerful but sinuous, speed almost inhuman execution ... mmm ... who knows how many things we can get him to try. "

Member 231 intervenes.

"Well, without further paperwork, here is the original."

Modified humans carry a cage. Inside, Monica is wearing a purple swimsuit. It is chained at the wrists, ankles and with a collar attached to the top of the cage, with little possibility of movement. Bandaged and with a refractor in the mouth.

"I gagged her, she is rebellious, I don't want her to offend my dear companions. She has already offended me, but I am not susceptible ... well, also because I know what awaits her."

Monica realizes that she is being watched by several people, but feigns indifference.

Paul takes an electric stinger and punches her right buttock, causing the guinea pig to gasp as she begins to retreat. The chains, although thick and secure, allow freedom of movement by bringing the abdomen closer to the front of the cage; but there Sonia waits for her, she too with a stinger, and hits her in the abdomen, making her retreat.

The others join in the game and for Monica the situation becomes "urgent" to say the least. They tease her in turn, from each side of the cage, sometimes at short intervals, sometimes with sadistic pauses, without saying a word.

The stingers are not particularly painful, especially for a robust and healthy specimen like her, but they are very annoying and, above all, cause uncontrolled movements of the body, offering a beautiful spectacle to the torturers.

The one-piece swimsuit adds a splash of color to your persona, yet leaves little room for the imagination of sadistic onlookers. Samantha appreciates how her body, when moving, creates very sensual muscle dynamics, things that could not be noticed in the photo.

After several minutes Monica begins to get angry and squirm like wild fury, forgetting that she had proposed to contain her emotions and frustrations so as not to give satisfaction to whoever was torturing her.

Paul sadistically activates the stinger in the inner thigh with a prolonged action for a few seconds, obtaining a grunt stifled by the bite. The noise of chains touching each other and the sight of them wrapping that living work of art are a boon to sadistic torturers.

Monica is exhausted. Her anger turns to frustration and she can't hold back the tears. Despite this, the stingers touch her again and again, inexorably. Now his chest rises and falls convulsively, out of control.

"Stop."

Member 231 orders the guinea pig to be brought to the center of the table around which colleagues are seated.

"Dear colleagues, here is the program for the first weeks: every morning Monica will train, she will keep in shape according to the procedure; In the afternoon we will do all kinds of tests, especially the first week; at night, already imagining that everyone wants to have it, the first turn will be ours ... to be my toy, right bitch? "

He taunts her again with his stinger. Monica emits a "nnnggghhhhh" of rage, especially at the word "toy", not knowing what to expect, and begins to pull the chains. Being a bit sweaty, her body looks even more animalistic.

"We will have to prepare a calendar ... ah, assuming that I, Robert, Sonia and Paul want to, you two, Julia and Samantha? What do you think? You can also continue with the boys, if you want, nobody forces you"

"Look, Member 231, as I said before ... this I think I can say with absolute certainty that, for the first time, we will be interested in the female body; this surpasses any other guinea pig we have had."

Saying that, Samantha runs a finger from the navel to the shackled dog's armpit causing her another uncontrolled reaction and a choked "nnggrrrrr".

"The barking bitch does not bite; look at her body, she looks like a savage"

Member 231 continues.

"So, on Monday Julia and Samantha, on Tuesday Paul, on Wednesday rest (after Paul I would very much like to see if he is still bragging), on Thursday I, Friday Robert, Saturday Sonia, Sunday rest. I think for the first week it could be like this. Today we will give you a test of your ... physical abilities, right, doggy? "

Touch, touch from behind on the buttocks with the consequent start of Monica.

Exercise routine
"nnnggghhhhh"
Monica gasps as the modified humans remove her gag.

Now it is outdoors; for the first time he realizes that he is really on an island; the sight of the sea around Monica has a desperate start.

But now you have to find out what's going on.

There are other people dressed like her, even in different colored swimsuits, women in bikinis or like her in a one-piece swimsuit, men, with briefs. They seem to be physically strong people, athletes of various kinds. They are surrounded by armed modified humans, a hallway that resembles an open cage. From her position, Monica can see that the corridor - cage continues as far as the eye can see.

Not far away, a naked man is X-tied in the open air, to a slowly rotating mechanism, exposing him fully to the sun. Monica freaks out and her blood runs cold at the thought of what they might do to her.

Member 231 appears, along with the two idiots and others outside the cage.

"Good morning, guinea pigs."

"Hello, Member 231"

The guinea pigs respond in chorus, frightened, Monica excluded.

"Didn't they teach you how to say hello, bitch?"

Monica stands still with a proud look.

"You know that your strength here won't help you, right?"

She nods her head and eight modified humans approach her inside the cage with their weapons pointed.

Monica looks at the unfortunate man who is forcibly kept out in the sun and renounces pride.

"Good morning Member 231"

"But hey, we're learning good manners; you're not as stupid as you sound, bitch ..."

Monica has an instinctive move to run toward the fence, groping to climb it and hit it again, but as soon as she hints at a move, the modified humans block her path and point their weapons at her.

Member 231 smirks.

"For those who are not familiar with the rules - a wink to Monica - there are five men and five women, plus another ten who have just finished, but who have no idea how long they have already done ... you will do a lap of three kilometers. We will start in random order, they will be timed. On each lap, the slowest man and woman will stop and they will be considered last classified. For the rest, again the same, every three kilometers there is an elimination. The classification is made in the order of elimination and then by the times It goes without saying that the last three will be used ... for unpleasant experiments, from the seventh to the fourth ... nothing to do, the second and third a day off and the first ... a whole week off"

Monica feels the tension in the other "competitors". It is the fourth to leave.

You don't know what strategy to adopt; she seemed to understand that everyone is an athlete; He has to compete with the women, some of whom had a more massive physique, for short races; in these it can prevail over long distances, but it is afraid of being eliminated in the first three kilometers. So, without too many calculations, he focuses on being part of a great career.

In the first kilometer, Monica realizes that the man who came after her is catching up. This should not be a problem, as she is competing with women, but it is the first time that a man has followed her and goes even faster than her; perhaps the other prisoners have been "taken" from the world of athletics; Furthermore, the way they are maintained and trained each day could increase their performance. Therefore, she begins to accelerate, a little scared and fearful by the so-called "experiments". The man no longer approaches her and maintains a constant distance. At the end of the tour of the island, he sees the figure of a man whom he has almost reached. Upon arrival at the finish line, the modified humans are prepared and the others are with timers and computers. After the finish line, the modified humans stop him with their pointed weapons; they immobilize the man in front of her and push him out of the way; it seems to him that he is terrified and crying. Obviously he is the first to be eliminated and being certainly the last or the penultimate he knows what to expect. Monica, thinking that she will no longer be one of the last, takes the last meters with a calmer speed to prepare for a distance race.

The moment of truth: you pass the goal ... you do not see any particular movements, you can continue. Now you understand the cruelty of the game: having to run without reference and always at your best. The rush taken at the end of the lap tired her a bit, but she regains strength and consciousness by thinking of all her workouts done in the past, and by thinking that she, after all, is Monica G. With her breathing he recovers and begins to pick up his pace. After the second lap she is still in the race and this consoles her given the fear that she escaped of what could happen to her; Besides, the man who was reaching her is no longer approaching her, a good sign. Now he is getting closer to the idea of being able to win at least one day of freedom.

Poor naive, Monica doesn't realize what is happening in the time trial zone. Member 231 watches the timing data in disbelief along with the others: After a first lap in line with the other guinea pigs, Monica was the fastest in the second round, even ahead of the men; In the third lap it is the only one that has lowered the times instead of increasing them; his pace is admired by all: an excellent career, which does not seem to cause him the slightest fatigue; only after the first six kilometers do you begin to see sweat on his magnificent body, which embellishes his already splendid and slender forms. Member 231 addresses his colleagues:

"As you can see, what is said about her seems to be true, at least in the race; as it is an example beyond all parameters, then she will compete in the pool, despite the procedures that prohibit two races on the same day; here she could win easily, without even getting too tired, but we'll have her believe she finished fourth ... there's no way to give her a day off, I'm really looking forward to trying it. "

On the fourth lap, Monica feels the first signs of fatigue, but her race is going well and she sees the possibility of earning a well-deserved rest.

But on the fourth lap they stop her, with a bit of astonishment: is it possible that someone has been faster?

"Well, bitch, as the first day is not bad. By a hair you did not finish third ... patience, it will be for another time"

They immobilize her and take her inside the detention center, to her cell. Water at will and some food supplements.

After fifteen minutes of total rest, Robert and Sonia approach the cell alone.

"Hello Monica"

Robert begins.

Sonia observes, without greeting her, the body from head to toe in her one-piece swimsuit.

"Be careful bitch"

Robert smiles.

Monica, despite the ten miles at breakneck speed, still has some energy. He throws himself with all his might on the glass, kicks and punches, screams and lunges at the two former teammates.

"Damn it! What do you want from me? They will never get me, but I will kill myself first! Do you understand, you monster of nature? And you psychopath? You will never have me!"

In response, Sonia flips the switch that raises the temperature, with the cell divided into two parts and the water flowing from a shower.

Monica starts to sweat, the heat becomes unbearable after a few minutes.

Sonia turns to the frightened Robert:

"Don't worry, she loves life too much to commit suicide, one thing is the words spoken by an angry beast, one thing is to be killed seriously ... you know, I know her ... well, quite intimately"

Monica, when she feels the temperature rise again, realizes that hers is a losing battle.

"Okay, that's enough, I'll do whatever you want, just tell me how to end this"

"Pay attention bitch"

Monica does, with tears in her eyes.

Sonia presses a button, turns the heat down, raises the grill, and Monica heads for the water.

"High"

"But how did I not do what you wanted?"

"Not yet bitch; you have to change for the next race; take off your swimsuit."

Monica does it reluctantly.

"Put your swimsuit in the slot. Good. Now turn to us, kneel down and put your hands on your head."

From the glass, Robert and Sonia look at their kneeling prisoner.

Robert intervenes, until that moment he had remained on the sidelines leaving the reins of the game to Sonia.

"I'd rather you be standing ... bitch"

Monica blushes; Until that moment, Robert had seemed friendly.

Robert, you can't suppress a sadistic smile. He is getting over his shyness towards his former love. Now she is naked, standing and at his mercy. You can see his muscles in every inch, his chest throbbing. The guinea pig's physical strength is useless against the island's restraint systems, the contrast between her and the two is further accentuated by her nudity and the fact that she dominates them in stature.

"Well, well, soon we will be able to study your body and without haste, now turn around, show us your firm ass"

Surprised Monica turns around with all her majesty. Seen from behind, it highlights the firmness of the long legs, buttocks and back. The arm muscles seen from behind are a living sculpture and move like arrows.

"Spread your legs and lean forward, now, resting your arms on the floor"

Monica feels herself blush when she feels a cold object like the ground in her hands.

The moment he leans in, he feels vulnerable to the sight of both of them in all their privacy. The abundant breasts stand out between the thighs, the legs are straight thanks to an unusual flexibility. The two are left with the knowledge that it will soon be fully available.

Monica, in that position, after intense physical activity and fatigue, feels a strange heat coming from her stomach; a strange sensation of pleasure takes over her.

"How is it possible?"

They both wonder.

Sonia and Robert look at each other a bit surprised, almost reading each other's minds, trapped by the doubt of a possible liking on their part.

Sonia intervenes

"Well, you can go cool off."

Monica, instead of feeling relieved, is almost reluctant to leave the post, but quickly dismisses the idea and heads for the stream of water, cooling off.

Fantastic Girl

The next test is done in a bikini, with a red top and blue panties, the kind of rather restrained, deliberately tight to highlight her breasts and nipples that, thanks to the fresh air, were quite evident.

It is in a pool with a two meter high edge, to avoid any escape attempt. There are men and women as in the previous race, the rules are the same, with the laps covered as a parameter.

After ten laps, the first one is eliminated. A woman, frightened by the prospect of the experiments she was about to undergo, has the unhealthy idea of trying to escape once she gets out of the pool. Being very physically strong, she manages to defeat six modified humans despite the handcuffs on her wrists, before being stunned by the strange weapons.

Monica doesn't stop too long and tries to do her best, despite the ten-mile run she just did. Swimming is one of the things he does best.

Member 231 observes the schedules as usual and notices the same trend that was already evident in the race: the girl seems to improve with the passage of time. Here too, after the quiet start, she starts to be even faster than men. And even here, it was decided to "get" her fifth, despite the clear possibility of being able to see her on the top step of the podium, even better than the men already after the first race.

Monica is, even here, a bit surprised, but for now she's content that she didn't finish in the bottom three places.

But the idea of escaping came to him after seeing the previous swimmer's attempt.

He realized that next to the pool there is a helicopter location and maybe ...

That idea makes her emboldened and taking advantage of the line that is going to be made with the swimmers and before they chain her again, she is going to take advantage of the last opportunity she thinks she may have before what awaits her at night with Member 231, to try to go to the helicopter.

She knocks down the two modified humans that surround her and goes straight like an arrow towards Member 231 who is surprised by the quick reaction of the woman.

At this time she is becoming a Fantastic Girl again.

He takes advantage of a post that he picks up from the ground and with its help plants it on the ground and with an incredible jump he passes over the guards that Member 231 has sent in his capture after the first surprise reaction, and lands next to her , giving her a new kick in the face and immobilizing her.

"How someone approaches me I kill her right here, damn!

Member 231 gestures to the modified humans to stay away.

"Now what are you going to do, bitch? I was starting to like you but after this you're going to suffer more than you can imagine, bitch "

"Shut up damn or I'll break your neck right now, let's go quietly to the helicopter ..."

Member 231 realizes that there is a real possibility that her plan will work by holding her hostage and how strong she is even after two grueling tests....

So try to distract her ...

"Look... there are Sonia and Robert, don't you want to tell them something?

Monica looks for a moment where Member 231 points so she takes the opportunity to try to get away, but the force with which she holds her is such that Monica immediately realizes the maneuver and punches her in the stomach.

"The next time you want to try to trick me I'll kill you, bitch. Where is the helicopter pilot? Call him to come and prepare it "

Member 231 does as she is told, so in a few moments a person dressed in military clothing appears next to the helicopter and enters to put it into operation.

In that Sonia and Robert are already next to them with faces difficult to decipher, but they seem confused.

"Member 231 what's going on here?"

Monica looks at them with such hatred that they recoil, but not enough ...

Even with Member 231 supported with one arm Monica throws a deadly leg towards them hitting Sonia directly in the neck. This falls struck down to the ground, dead on the spot.

Robert is paralyzed in surprise and horror at seeing his friend drop dead, allowing Monica to launch another kick at him this time in the genitals with such superhuman force that Robert lets out an inhuman screech of pain and rubs himself at it. floor.

"This is to make your eggs stop working for good, you fucking sadist"

And with one swift movement he gets into the helicopter, already underway, behind Member 231 which he has pushed inside.

"Well, you can imagine what I want so order it!"

"Pilot, let's go to the mainland"

The helicopter begins to rise allowing Monica to breathe again, she had realized that she had been holding her breath for a long time, and she begins to see that she was getting out of that hell.

When the helicopter is already over the sea a few miles from the island, Monica, Fantastic Girl, turns to Member 231 ...

"Bitch, it was nice meeting you ..."

And throws it into the sea ...

THE UNDRESSING GAME

125

Paul and I had gone to a party given by friends of his.

He didn't know almost anyone, but they seemed like a nice bunch.

Paul apologized and started talking to some teammates he hadn't seen since the race ended, so I was left alone.

I poured myself some sangria and began to drink calmly, looking around for someone I knew.

Everyone was busy talking to someone and he didn't want to interrupt any conversation.

Suddenly, I saw a couple of people slip through the door at the back of the room.

Before long, three more people entered as well.

Then one more.

That was too much for my curiosity, so I decided to see what was going on in there.

I opened the door and saw a large group of people look towards the center of the room.

I stood on tiptoe to see what they were looking at and discovered a boy in his early twenties sitting on a table with a box full of little cards in his hand.

People laughed incessantly and it piqued my curiosity even more.

I decided to ask someone to find out.

I tapped a girl in front of me on the shoulder.

"Hey, sorry. What is all this? I asked, raising my voice above the laughter.

"We are playing" Do you dare? " "He replied" Do you want to play?

"I don't know how to play" I said.

"It doesn't matter, I'll explain it to you right now," he exclaimed. You'll see how easy it is. When your turn comes you must choose a card from the box that the 'moderator' of the game carries, which is the boy on the table. There is a "challenge" written on the card that you must meet. If you decide not to comply, you must pay a pledge. You must take off some clothes.

" I understand. That's why there is that one there without a shirt "I said pointing to a man who was laughing. "

"That's it" she replied "It's that we've been playing for a while. In addition to that there are others who have already paid a pledge. That girl is already in her panties and I had to take off my shoes. "

I looked down at his feet and saw that he was telling the truth.

I smiled, thanked him, and left the room.

I looked for Paul to ask if he wanted to come in and play with me.

"No darling" he replied "You see if you want, I'm talking to some friends from the university."

I went in alone.

They told me that to enter the game I had to first tell the moderator.

I did so and when it was my turn I took out a card.

"With a blindfold, kiss three members of the opposite sex and then guess who is who."

They chose three men, and they blindfolded me.

The first seemed like he wanted to reach my tonsils with his tongue.

The second used his tongue less, but spent almost a minute rubbing my ass while kissing me.

The third also used his tongue a lot and not only rubbed my ass, but also stroked my tits.

I let them do it because if I had stopped any of them they would have eliminated me.

I took off the blindfold and hit all three, one for his beard, and the other two for height.

When it was my turn again, there was already a woman in a bra and panties, and a man in his underpants.

I took out a new card.

"You'll have to show your underwear to the one who can match its color. Three people can test."

What a bad luck! She was wearing a garter belt and matching black panties.

Surely someone would think of saying that color.

But the worst thing was that the panties were transparent and I could see everything through them.

Why wouldn't I have worn the maroon panties?

They chose three other men.

The first said he was not wearing anything.

I laughed and told him that he had failed.

The second said it was black.

Bingo! You got it right!

I told him to turn around and lifted my dress so that only he could see her.

Seeing me, he whistled gratefully.

The moderator of the game said that since I had lost I had to remove some garment.

With a sensual gesture I put my hands under my skirt, lowered my panties and hung them on the hanger with the rest of the clothes that the others had already removed.

On the next shift, two men lost their pants and one woman their bra, and two people left the game with only ten people left.

The topless woman reminded the group that I had not done the same number of tests as the rest of the people and suggested that I have two extra tests to put me on the same level as the others.

People ignored my protests and quickly voted to give me two extra tests in a row.

I took out the first card.

"Take off your bra without opening any buttons on your dress or blouse."

As my bra opened in the front, I opened it without any problem and passed one side under each of my arms.

Meanwhile, everyone was staring at me and I heard some people comment that everything was transparent to me.

The moderator said that one of the rules of the game prohibited wearing any garment again.

I took out a new card.

"Choose three people of the same sex with the straw game. French kiss one that lasts at least a minute."

I broke three matches, mixed them with a few others and passed them around so that each woman could choose one.

The one who got one of the three broken matches would have a prize.

Joanna, a red-haired girl in her twenties, a body with perfect curves and a little shorter than me, was the first to take one of them out.

He laughed and said that he had always been good at that game.

He made me sit on his knees and the moderator reminded me that if I interrupted the kiss I would lose the challenge.

Joanna began to kiss me with great determination and, knowing that I had nothing under my clothes, first she caressed my breasts and then she slid a hand under my skirt, leaving it just above my pubis, playing with my clit.

I endured the kiss, but couldn't continue to sit with those experienced hands on my clit.

Expertly, he made me reach an orgasm, while I squirmed on his knees.

When I broke off the kiss, the group clapped and I saw that six minutes had passed.

Joanna still kept her hand on my throbbing pussy for a moment and then I got up.

However, he did not stop pressing on him until I took a few steps away.

My breathing was fast and I started to wait for my turn to come again.

A man lost his boxer shorts revealing a thick, hard cock.

A second woman lost her bra.

The woman who no longer had a bra lost her skirt, leaving nothing on.

I wondered what would happen if they lost again.

Paul chose this moment to enter the room.

The moderator asked him if he wanted to stay.

He took a look at the two women's boobs and didn't hesitate to say yes.

They told him that he had to accept five challenges if he wanted to stay.

He pulled out his first card.

"With a blindfold, kiss three members of the opposite sex and then guess who is who."

I was the second and Joanna the third.

I rubbed Paul like the first woman had done, rubbing his cock through his pants.

Joanna did better, pulling down his fly and reaching inside.

Paul didn't hit me (he thought I was number one).

He lost four of the five garments by standing there in his boxers, with a tremendous erection struggling to free himself.

The moderator announced that things had gone far enough and that it was time to draw the strongest cards.

I got the first one.

They blindfolded me and put three cocks in my hands.

He had to guess who each belonged to.

Incredibly I was unable to distinguish Paul's from the others.

With all the people in the room watching, I took off my blouse.

The woman who was already naked from the previous round lost her challenge and all the men pulled a straw.

The moderator told the woman that she would have to sit on the dick of the one who drew the shorter straw for at least five minutes.

I watched her sit on top of the winner as he carefully thrust his cock into her dripping hole, wondering if my punishment would be the same if I got naked.

The moderator began to count the time.

She tried to behave like nothing, as if by not moving she was going to convince us that she was not being fucked there in the middle of everyone, but the slow movements with which the man penetrated her made, after about three minutes, begin to react.

She was starting to get into the matter when the moderator said that time was up and made her get up, to which she refused, holding tightly to the owner of the cock that was giving her so much pleasure.

We all laughed at that amused reaction, while Joanna and the moderator tried to remove that erect member from her hungry cunt.

They barely succeeded.

The next was me.

"Look at the boobs of three women and then, blindfolded, identify them by touching them only with your tongue."

Joanna quickly volunteered as well as two other women.

I looked at their boobs, gauging their size and features, and then they blindfolded me.

My tongue would take turns exploring each of the tits.

It occurred to me that if I licked them eagerly they would end up emitting some sound of pleasure that would help me know who each one was.

The second was silent until my teeth brushed her nipple and she couldn't help a moan of pleasure.

The third moaned at the first lick.

I said Joanna was the first, and then who did she think the other two were.

I got it right.

I already believed that the challenge had passed when the moderator said that he had to serve a punishment.

He had realized that he had used his teeth on one of them.

He told me to take off my skirt.

He was going to say to keep undressing me, but stopped when he saw my hot red and black garter belt.

He told me that I could continue with my skirt on, but that from now on I would have to serve the same penalties as the players who were already naked.

He reached into the punishment box and pulled out a card.

He didn't show it to me, but he had the three remaining women read it.

They approached me, circled me slowly, and carried me to the bed.

Joanna sat on it and the other two put me on their knees.

The woman whose nipple had been bitten positioned close to my head so that my face rested on her pussy.

He held my arms so I couldn't move.

The other held my legs and began to play with my pussy.

"Did you see how wet she is, Joanna? "I heard him say.

Meanwhile, he began to touch my clitoris with one finger and explore my interior with another at the same time.

Involuntarily my hips began to squirm on Joanna's knees.

Suddenly, it hit me hard.

I did not complain, for I was afraid I would miss the punishment.

It hit me a few more times and finally stopped.

"How many have there been? "I wonder.

"I don't know" I answered scared.

"Then we will start again" he said.

Joanna kept whipping me hard while my pussy was explored by the other girl.

This time I looked at counting the spankings.

When he was twenty he stopped and looked at the woman holding my arms.

"Has he already started licking you? He asked.

" I do not answer.

"We will start again" exclaimed Joanna.

I quickly buried my face in that pussy that belonged to a woman who, as you may have already realized, did not even know her name.

Joanna kept hitting me harder and harder.

At last, he stopped.

I had counted 23 lashes this time, although I was afraid I had missed some.

"How many have they been? He asked me again.

"Twenty-five" I said to make sure.

"No, you will have to do better" said Joanna "We will start again.

The rest of the people applauded and cheered incessantly, but not me but my torturers.

I also heard Paul congratulate Joanna on the show she was making me put on.

During all that time, the hands that played with my pussy had not slowed one iota.

I had already lost count of my orgasms, (there had been at least five), and judging by the number of times the woman I was eating her pussy had grabbed my head, she had had at least three.

Joanna stopped her blows once more.

"How many have they been? "I wonder.

"Twenty-five" I said again, preparing for a new thrashing.

"Right" he said without further ado.

Then, addressing the woman in my head, he asked:

"Virginia, has it satisfied you?

"At the moment yes" I heard her answer "Unless she grows a cock ..."

"And you, Julia? He asked the one who had been exploring my pussy.

"Yes" he answered with heavy breathing "For me, that's okay."

I started to get up, but Joanna stopped me and made me lie down.

"They may be done, but I didn't" tell me "Now you must count the next ten strokes so that everyone in this room can hear you. Then you will kiss me, Virginia and Julia's pussies as a way of thanking you for how much fun you've had with us. "

I accepted.

It took him over a minute to hit me all ten times.

Then I kissed Virginia's pussy without even getting up and thanked her.

I got up and kissed Julia's pussy and thanked her too, saving Joanna for last.

The pussy eating I dedicated to her lasted about three minutes, until I finally felt her come.

Then I also thanked him.

As he did so, I realized that he meant what he was saying.

The experience had been most gratifying.

Now it was Paul's turn ...

Paul picked out a challenge card and I could tell from the look on his face that he hadn't gotten what he expected.

"Using only the mouth and blindfolded, identify the cocks of three men."

"I'm not going to do this" he said, turning to me.

"Wait a minute" I replied somewhat annoyed "You have had a great time watching how I was riding with three women and now you don't want to do this. I think you are being unfair. "

"But, is that ..." he began to say "Is that they are ... dicks !!"

"Come on" I said, seeing that I was already convincing him "Nothing will happen to you if you do, it will not do you any harm. Also, think about the punishment that the moderator will give you if you refuse. "

I'm not sure which of my arguments finally managed to convince him, the point is that, after thinking about it for a moment more, he announced that he was going to try.

I looked closely at the three cocks exposed before Paul.

He was blindfolded and was shaking from head to toe.

I tried to cheer him up by telling him that this was turning me on tremendously, which was completely true.

At last he made up his mind and began to meet the challenge.

In the end it was not so bad, it finished in less than a minute and only hit one.

The moderator asked me to help him choose the punishment.

With his eyes still blindfolded, they made him sit on the edge of the bed.

The women still in the room undressed.

From that moment on, the clothes would no longer serve as punishment.

Each of them sat on his stiff cock for exactly one minute.

I was the fourth and Paul recognized me from the stockings I was still wearing or maybe something else.

He begged me to stay a little longer, long enough to come.

I gave him a kiss that unclogged his throat and sat on him for a few more moments while his hips pushed me over and over again, trying to reach orgasm quickly.

I did not allow it.

At the end of the day it was a punishment, so I got up leaving him halfway.

Joanna was the last to insert his cock.

She aroused him mercilessly and also left him before he came to come.

"If you need me to choose another punishment, do not hesitate to consult me" I offered to the moderator, while Paul got up and took off, exhausted, the blindfold.

"Don't worry" he smiled at me "From now on we will choose between the two of them."

I saw Joanna take the next card.

He read it to himself and it seemed amusing.

We asked him to read it aloud and he did.

"Choose three men and touch their cocks. Then, blindfolded, sit on them and identify their owners."

She paced the room and chose two men, oddly, the ones with the biggest cocks.

When she reached Paul, she stopped in front of him and gently took his cock.

Paul took a step forward, happy because now he was going to have the chance to finish what we hadn't left him before.

But, Joanna released her, smiling cruelly.

"For now you've had enough" he said "If you're good, maybe I'll choose you for another game."

And she walked away from him, leaving him with a stiff cock and a disappointed scowl on his face.

I couldn't help but smile.

It served him well.

Joanna chose the third and brought him along with the other two.

She touched each of the cocks until they were hard and when she was finished she was blindfolded.

Then he impaled himself on each of them, without giving any of the three a chance to come.

She did come hard on the third cock.

Incomprehensibly, none of them were right.

We all realized that I had failed on purpose, even the moderator who called me to deliberate.

Finally, we found a punishment according to Joanna's personality, although deep down we all knew that more than a punishment, it was a gift for her.

We tied Joanna to the bed face down, so that her waist was bent at the edge, leaving her on her knees with her ass exposed to all of us.

The punishment would consist of each man fucking her from behind for exactly one minute.

I would be by her side to introduce each of the cocks to her.

The moderator would take time.

A gesture of his would be the signal that time was up and that they should remove his cock.

If they refused, I would be the one in charge of removing it by force (taking them by the eggs if necessary).

I went up to Paul and said something in his ear.

Then I took my place.

I grabbed the first of the six cocks that were going to enter Joanna's hole with both hands.

"The tip is a bit dry" I lied, because all that was making me the most horny "I think I'm going to have to moisten it with my tongue."

I did so, recreating more than necessary, which earned me a reprimand from the moderator.

Then, I expertly introduced it.

Just as Joanna started to move in time with her partner, the moderator gave me the signal to stop.

I grabbed his cock gently and pulled it out quickly.

I also moistened the second with my warm mouth, as, as I said, it was 'necessary'.

When I put it in, his cock began to move in and out at lightning speed.

Despite that, I pulled her out before she could achieve any satisfaction.

The third and the fourth passed in the same way.

The moderator was the fifth.

I looked at his cock and slowly shook my head.

"I think I'm going to have to wet this cock too" I said maliciously.

I put it in my mouth and began to lick and suck it as if there was no one else in the room.

I devoted more time to it than to any other.

At last, he stopped me with his hand.

"I think enough is enough" he said, gasping with excitement.

"Are you sure you want me to stop? I asked sensually.

"For now yes" he told me "Later I may let you continue.

The moderator was exactly one minute and was the one who came closest to cumming, because of the excitement that my cock eating had caused him.

Paul was the last.

Joanna had pushed her hips hard against the last two cocks, trying to orgasm, but not succeeding.

I decided that I would make her suffer a little more before the last attack.

I slowly parted the lips of her pussy with the excuse that this way the cock would enter more easily.

That made Joanna shudder with pleasure.

Then my finger slid all over her clit, arousing her even more.

I thought enough was enough and let Paul come closer.

He shoved her in, as Joanna's pussy was more than lubricated.

He started giving him powerful thrusts like the others had done, but after the fourth, I took it off him and made him shove it up his ass.

Just at the end of the minute of rigor, the moderator gave me the signal to remove it.

Joanna pushed back with her hips to try to keep the swollen member in place, but was unsuccessful.

The moderator stared at me.

"Now we will vote to decide the punishment we impose on you" he told me, speaking out loud so that the whole world could hear him.

" Punishment? To me? But why? I said, incredulous.

"For having changed the rules of the previous game" he replied "The cocks could only enter her pussy and not her ass. Besides, you weren't allowed to eat all the cocks without my permission ".

Nobody voted against.

Meanwhile, I watched Joanna roll onto her back, her hand slowly floating to her hungry clit.

The people had come to a decision.

"We are going to blindfold you and then we will all do what we want without you knowing who did what" exclaimed the moderator, smiling.

Suddenly, someone put a blindfold over my eyes and several hands pushed me onto the bed.

A second later, a cock entered my mouth and I began to suck it eagerly.

A second cock dug into my dripping cunt, but after four thrusts, it came out.

Then, I felt like someone separated my buttocks and immediately afterwards, another cock (or maybe the same one) entered my ass with a single push.

I wanted to scream but the cock that had buried in my mouth stopped me.

They slowly put me on my side, so that neither of the cocks that were fucking me nor the two mouths that were starting to suck my tits would get away from their targets.

I noticed that at least one of them was a woman's because her facial skin was very soft, without a trace of a beard.

Several people crowded around my sex and tried to penetrate me.

After a slight struggle, one of them succeeded.

Such was the fight that had formed between the people between my legs, that I felt as if several people were fucking me at the same time.

It was as if all the people had gotten on top of me.

The cock in my mouth went in and out of her relentlessly, while the cock in my pussy kept pumping, but with some difficulty.

The one on my ass still penetrated me, but it seemed that most of the stimulation from its owner came from my efforts to counter the thrusts of everyone else.

Apparently the two people who were sucking on my boobs had decided to turn me on and stimulate me as much as I could handle.

The truth is that I was glad I was blindfolded, so I could fully concentrate on what they were doing to me.

Seeing what was happening would only have served as a distraction.

One of the girls took my hand, put it on her pussy and started rubbing herself with my fingers, using them to masturbate.

She was so confused by everything that she couldn't react.

It was as if I had become an object, as if I had been deprived of my will.

The cock in my mouth began to throb.

Seconds later, a stream of milk shot up my throat.

I tried to swallow it all, but some fell down my cheek.

Before I could recover, they put a pussy in its place, which I began to lick without delay.

Apparently the two who were fucking my pussy and my ass had found a common rhythm.

With their thrusts they got me to come.

I was in the middle of my second orgasm, when I heard a scream and the man who was driving my pussy came.

Then, as he slowly withdrew, I felt his cum slowly start to flow out of my hole.

His partner, fully dedicated to my ass, kept pumping even harder.

A face appeared on my pussy and began to lick it passionately.

The feeling of being fucked in the ass while someone else was eating my pussy was new to me.

I started to cum again.

Someone started pulling my hair.

Despite the difficulty, I tried to keep complying with the demands of the pussy that was on my face.

A new cock appeared in my hand and I began to wiggle it up and down.

One of the mouths that was on my nipples disappeared, taking its place a pair of strong hands that began to scrub my tits, kneading them as if they were bread dough.

"I think this girl wants to get spanked a few times" said a voice to my right that I couldn't figure out whose it was.

The pussy I was sucking pressed even closer to my face.

I licked it as well as I could.

Her thighs crushed my head as I reached orgasm.

Quickly a new cock replaced it and worked its way into my mouth.

I imagined a line of people queuing at each of my attractions, waiting for their turn.

I realized that I had lost all connection between those sexual organs and the people to whom they were attached.

The blindfold had taken away everything except my ability to feel what was happening.

I had to admit that from the moment I walked into that room, I had been secretly hoping that something like this might happen.

The truth was that, since Joanna first aroused my clit with her fingers, she had been in a state of constant arousal.

Apparently the man who was fucking me had finally reached the point of no return.

He grabbed my hips and took command of my movements.

Seconds later, I felt how large jets of semen were launched from his cock into my insides.

Then he lay down next to me and I felt his cock soften, slowly coming out of my ass.

Immediately after, he was gone, leaving my rear end free.

The mouth of my right tit was replaced by another strong hand. Now my boobs were being massaged as a team.

Suddenly one of the hands disappeared.

Seconds later I noticed something in my chest, in the valley formed by my two tits.

It was a hand, a hand smeared with some kind of lubricant.

He went over my tits over and over again, smearing them with that slimy liquid.

Someone got on my belly, climbed up my body and placed a hard cock between my lubricated tits.

His hands joined my breasts, turning them into a pussy ready to be fucked.

The man's hips began to move back and forth at an insane rate.

The cock in my mouth disappeared without firing its load down my throat and the cock in my hand was replaced by a fiery pussy.

Someone kissed me on the mouth, I think a woman, snaking her tongue down my throat.

I could feel the semen dripping from my ass and my pussy.

The cock that was fucking my tits increased its speed.

Someone lifted my legs, exposing my pussy.

They whipped me hard in the ass ten times, while one hand took a place on my pussy, masturbating me.

The cock on my chest began to spit semen with force.

It hit me in the face and then fell dripping off her.

He must also have reached the woman who was kissing me, but that did not stop him from sticking his tongue into me for a single second.

The already flaccid member moved away from my tits.

The kissing mouth moved away as well, as did the finger from my clit.

For a moment I just lay there, exhausted.

A minute or so later, the blindfold was removed.

They gave me a towel and I gently wiped myself with it as I watched the assembled group.

Among them was Paul, my boyfriend, who had also participated.

I realized that I had not recognized him among all those people giving me non-stop pleasure.

"Now you are going to thank each and every one of us for having provided you with such a pleasant time" the moderator told me "But you will do it in a very special way."

A few moments later he was kissing each of the women's pussies.

Then, I put each of the men's cocks in my mouth, thanking each of them.

Just then the door opened.

" Where is everybody? "Said the newcomer" Damn, I think I have the wrong room! "

SUBMISSIVE LATIN WOMAN

145

Juliet received further instructions in a letter.

It was a white envelope with "Confidential" written in bold.

Juliet's legs began to wobble before she could open the envelope.

He remembered talking to Paul last night.

What will your next bold plan be?

From their relationship over the past few months, she was gaining new insights about herself and her sexuality.

Before Paul was introduced, he thought he knew a lot about sex.

But since her relationship with Paul, she had started doing many things that she had never imagined before.

She had forgotten many of her misconceptions about herself.

Before meeting Paul, she thought she was completely satisfied with sex.

But she soon realized that she was not satisfied with what she was doing.

He had blindfolded her during their second date.

Julieta would never have imagined how sensitive our body can become when we cannot see.

Each limb was asymptomatic to the touch, and she was overcome with curiosity to know which point would be touched next on her body.

He felt that every touch of his body should last forever, and he was struggling to enjoy every touch.

The next time, Paul tied his limbs to the bed.

Feeling that we are helpless' emotionally, when we see our own naked body, our partner enjoying it, and we cannot do anything, we cannot resist, we cannot avoid anything ourselves, this feeling is very different.

You are using her beautiful, youthful body as you please, in front of your eyes ... and you just want to feel what it will do to you.

Mixed feelings of helplessness, and excitement.

They played these new games constantly and she enjoyed all those games to the fullest, appreciating Paul's creativity.

Interestingly, Juliet, who believed her nature to be aggressive and domineering, was easily giving up on Paul in the romance game.

Not only that, she loved giving herself completely, giving him her body, doing what he would do, doing what he told her to do.

She was beginning to feel that someone should dominate her, make her do anything.

This change in her nature had taken her by surprise.

Last night, Paul had said that tomorrow's daring would be the culmination of the game so far.

"You hear everything I say, don't you?" He had asked.

Submission had come to her just by asking.

"Yes, Lord, I'll do what you tell me," she answered quietly.

She could speak very softly, but this discovery began only when she met Paul.

"Well then, tomorrow you will receive a letter in your office. That letter will contain further instructions for you."

... and now he really had that letter in his hand!

With trembling hands, he broke the seal on the letter.

What would be written on it?

What will Paul's next bold plan be?

What would I have to do for him today?

A little scared, a little embarrassed too, she began to take out the white paper inside the envelope, behold and read ...

"Slave

1. Get ready for our game tonight at eight o'clock, be brave.

2. You should dress like this: soft red pants, matching blouse, matching panties-bra, gold earrings in the ears, silver belt and high-heeled shoes.

3. A Mercedes will pick you up at eight o'clock. The driver will know where to go. He will give you more instructions later. Just as you

follow my instructions now, you must also follow his instructions at night.

4. In addition, you will not take anything else since you will not need it. You don't need a bag or anything else. "

Julieta's chest throbbed with excitement until she finished reading the instructions.

Excited by what would happen today, she began to get wet.

Paul, a dress code, eight o'clock at night, Mercedes driver ... nothing more.

He always managed to distract her at work.

A little scary, a little excitement, a little fun, a lot of curiosity ...

Until now, however bold their games were, they had been played in 'private' locations.

Sometimes at Juliet's house, sometimes at Paul's apartment, and once at a hotel.

But she would surrender to Paul alone ... but today she would meet a third person, the driver of that Mercedes!

Has Paul given the driver some bold instructions?

Paul said, you must obey everything the driver says ...

What happens if the driver asks her to remove her clothes in the car?

Or if he asks her to kiss him sitting in the car?

Or if you tilt it while driving ... ??? Oh God

Why did she confess all this to Paul?

Did she make a mistake by trusting him so much?

On the one hand, with such doubts on her mind, she also believed that Paul would not allow any situation to arise that would put her in danger.

She smiled to herself, realizing that the idea of the driver forcing her to undress was as terrifying as it was exciting.

At eight o'clock, Juliet had dressed and undressed three times.

At first he wore red pants, but it wasn't soft.

I look good like this, why should I pay so much attention to him ...

While saying this, without realizing it, he had removed his pants and looked for a softer red.

Then he started looking for the gold earrings.

He had never had a chance to wear these earrings as he used to wear jeans and a T-shirt, but Paul had said once or twice that he liked them very much.

Oddly, she didn't remember when she had told Paul that she had a silver belt.

But he had written the same thing in his letter, so he must have known, that's for sure.

While mentally appreciating his intelligence ...

... The clock struck eight and a car honked on the road.

Julieta ran down the stairs and looked through the peephole in the front door.

In front of the gate was a long black Mercedes.

She pulled her bag off her shoulder and tossed it on the sofa in the hall, locked the front door, unlocked the gate, and walked over to the Mercedes.

The uniformed driver opened the back door for him.

The driver was middle-aged and educated in appearance.

She sat inside, wondering if he would already give her any instructions.

the driver very politely closed the door, sat down, and started the engine.

As expected, riding in a Mercedes was really comfortable, but he didn't seem to mind.

Now this driver will tell you what to do, how and if you really want to obey what he says ...

Many of those thoughts were churning in his mind.

The Mercedes sped through the busy city streets.

Little by little, the surrounding traffic became less dense and he realized that they had left the city and entered the industrial zone.

The factories and office buildings on either side of the narrow street did not seem familiar.

Suddenly, the driver slowed the Mercedes and entered a lot that appeared to be abandoned.

Although the vehicle speed was slow enough to enter from the main road, it was not slow enough to read the letters on the sign outside the parcel.

Inside the plot, Juliet sees a Vigilante's cabin with an old, dilapidated door.

The driver stopped the car and got out.

He came back and opened the door for Juliet.

As soon as she got out, he closed the door and grabbed her by the neck and led her to the collapsed Vigilante cabin.

Juliet had not yet heard the voice of the driver.

That four-by-four foot cabin had a counter at the front.

The young man sitting at the counter said to the driver:

"Thanks friend, see you next time."

The driver just smiled and quickly turned and left.

Now Julieta was alone in front of that unknown but handsome young man.

There was some magic in his smile.

"Juliet, isn't your name? Follow me," the young man ordered.

Juliet followed him carefully.

The two entered an office-like room at the rear of the half-ruined building.

There was nothing in the room but a table and chairs in the corner.

"Are you ready for today's unique adventure Juliet?" He asked getting serious.

"Uhm? Maybe ..." Juliet said getting a little nervous.

"Well," he said, smiling mysteriously, "to all who give you instructions tonight you will follow them carefully. Without any doubt ... and without asking anyone. Some of the suggestions will be strange or strange, but believe me, you will be happier. if you follow the instructions. Then do what you are told, without shame, fear or fear. "

"Okay. What do I have to do?" Juliet asked firmly.

Looking at Juliet's sexy body, he said:

"Listen then. First, take off your clothes."

"All?" Juliet asked hesitantly.

"No," she said with a mischievous smile, "take off everything except the panties, the earrings, the silver belt and the heels."

Juliet did not know if she had heard the instructions correctly.

He had given him instructions in very clear words and in a raised voice.

However, Juliet felt that he had not been able to say any of that.

Even after digesting his suggestion with great effort, she was still waiting for him to leave the room ...

She thought she should at least turn her back on him.

Of course, Juliet knew she was expecting a lot, but still ...

In a fit of rage, he pulled down his pants, leaving his belt on.

She unbuttoned the first button on her blouse and looked at him to show him that you are no less in this situation.

But as soon as she noticed her gaze slide down as she removed another button, she inadvertently looked down at herself.

She was embarrassed to see the very tight, soft pink bra that was clearly visible after two buttons came off the top.

Her fleshy, soft breasts struggling to get out of him.

Excited, she began to breathe harder and harder, and her already plump breasts seemed to swell.

Without wasting any more time, she unbuttoned all the missing buttons on her blouse.

As soon as he pulled the pants off her feet, she glanced at him, and pulled her belt-tight blouse off with both hands.

Then, pushing them back and of course puffing up her big and beautiful chest even more, she also removed the bra hooks.

But for a few moments she remained in the same pose and looked at him.

He stepped forward, looking at her swollen breasts.

Realizing that there was no escape, Juliet rolled her eyes, took a deep breath and slowly removed her bra with both hands.

She didn't have the courage to look him in the eye now.

And then he realized that he was still waiting for her to come out or turn her back on him.

But she could have turned her back herself when she was undressing in front of this strange young man!

But she had brazenly stripped off her clothes one by one in front of him ...

She was even more embarrassed by this thought.

"Fold your clothes and put them on the table," Julieta regained consciousness at his next suggestion.

She opened her eyes, but, avoiding his gaze, she picked up the pants, blouse, and bra that were rolling down her legs and walked over to the table.

Folding them carefully, she placed them on the table and stood in front of him, but not far behind.

"Now turn around and stand with both hands back," he instructed again in a serious voice.

Now, turning her back, wondering what it would be for, she turned and waved both hands back as if she had gotten very lazy.

She nodded, feeling him coming towards her.

Her delicate wrists were touched by cold metal as she thought about what would happen next.

What new thing is this, she asked, until something clicked and both hands were caught in the same pose he had told her.

Oh God. You are here in an unknown place, with an unknown man, at this moment, in such a state ... and now so defenseless !!

Few clothes on the body, no phone nearby, no bag ...

What use would they be for?

Both hands were trapped in shackles from behind.

Paul is not in sight.

And this strange but handsome young man is getting so close to you ... stupid!

You are stupid, Juliet.

Why do people believe so blindly?

And that also in a person like Paul ... how well do you know him?

What will happen to you now.

Oh God, what did I do ...

"Come on," he said, not waiting for her to walk, but holding onto her shackles and walking toward the door.

There was no point in protesting.

As soon as she was out the door, a blast of cold air swept over Juliet and tears welled up in her eyes.

He was walking with heavy steps.

He almost dragged her into the dark parking lot.

In such a half-naked state, he also felt the support of that darkness, but ...

But what is this?

The shame of her own semi-naked body, of her own helplessness, of the involuntary company of this young stranger, while she was afraid, also excited her helplessly.

She was ashamed to feel the sweet sensations that took place covered by the only garment that was left on her body.

She didn't know exactly what you were thinking.

Even though her body was cold, she felt warm as she left the room and into the parking lot, with the touch of her body as she walked and the strong grip of the shackle bar.

Her dark chocolate nipples tightened and began to ache from the cold air.

It looked like he was holding the bar with both hands very tightly ... but she had both hands trapped behind her back.

And then what would happen to him if he had both hands free.

If he pinched her stiff nipples with the same force that he held his barbell ...

Juliet was terribly surprised by her own thoughts.

What were you thinking a few moments ago?

Due to this helplessness, the shame, the tears had just reached her eyes.

Now the touch of the rocky hand of this unknown man should touch our most intimate part, the thought ... or the desire ...

God!

What happened to me

What thoughts come to mind?

Paul, where are you, evil?

You ... you made me like this!

Will I be able to look in the mirror tomorrow or not?

There was a small gate at the end of the parking lot.

The stranger opened the door and pushed Juliet inside.

It was like a big empty chamber.

Julieta narrowed her eyes and tried to look around, but it was all dark except for the lamp that hung in the middle of the room.

He pulled her up again and placed her under the lamplight.

Her beautiful body, which had been covered in darkness for so long, was exposed again.

Embarrassed and suddenly the light in her eyes, she wiped her eyes hard.

A few moments passed in extreme silence.

There is no movement, there is no movement.

I wonder if he left me here ...

She felt his touch brush on her linear waist.

Once or twice the touch moved slowly from both sides of her waist to her armpits and then slid down and slid down the edges of her panties.

Julieta wiped her eyes hard as if she knew what would happen next.

The fingers of both hands pulled down the edges of her pink panties.

Her panties caught when they reached her thighs.

With his hands tied behind his back, he couldn't do anything.

The fingers of his left hand came forward from behind with authority and began to lower the front of her panties, pinching them, touching her wet vagina.

In the next moment, the last garment on his body, although only nominally, fell at his feet.

"Put them aside," his powerful voice echoed through that void.

He released her legs from her panties without thinking.

Now she was completely naked, naked, naked.

Not to mention, there were a few things left on her handsome body: earrings, a silver belt, and high heels.

Of course, none of this served to avoid embarrassment, but she began to think of herself as she faced the situation she was in.

"Stay still there," she said, giving the next order.

Although Juliet opened her eyes now, she did not want to disobey him.

As he thought about what he was doing, he heard him push something.

She looked to the right and saw him.

He was pushing something with wheels towards her.

It was a table.

The table was roughly waist high.

Leather straps were strapped across the table.

He brought the table right in front of her.

Then, circling her again, he pushed her forward and bent her across the table.

"Spread your feet, Juliet," he ordered.

She obediently moved both legs slightly each to the side.

"More still," he yelled, and she stood with both legs wide open.

Now her wet vagina was touching the leather on the table.

As soon as her legs met the table legs, he bound both her legs tightly with the leather straps.

Now it was impossible for him to move.

Surrounding her, he freed her hands from the shackles.

He smiled and stood in front of her.

As she looked at her naked body, Juliet's eyes automatically lowered in embarrassment.

He kept giving orders.

"Get down and touch your toes."

When she leaned down, he leaned forward and tied her hands to her legs.

No matter how brave she was, Juliet was terrified by this state of helplessness.

At this stage, she was unable to move on her own.

Her wet vagina and full buttocks were completely exposed in front of 'that' stranger.

Not only that, but her vagina, and even her ass hole, must have been visible to him now.

She was trying to control her breathing, wondering what he would do next.

For a minute she didn't notice any movement from him, but then she realized that he was very close behind her.

And at the same time he felt a very familiar touch, but in an unexpected place ...

Vaseline! Yes, it was petroleum jelly.

He rubbed petroleum jelly into her rear hole with a coated finger.

He spread it around her for a while and then inserted his finger into her anus.

Juliet held her breath for a moment.

Before meeting Paul, she was not aware of any other use for her anal hole other than usual.

She used to feel upset when she saw anal sex in a porn video with Paul.

He would yell at Paul and force him to pass the scene.

But once he had tied her arms and legs to the bed and taught her the type of dominant sex, he had inserted a rubber plug into her anus, despite her opposition.

Juliet, who was initially screaming, accepted this kind of fun in no time.

After that, every time Paul came down to lick her vagina, she would start begging him to insert at least one finger behind her.

In fact, Paul really liked doing it like this, but just to annoy Juliet, he used to remind her of his rejection and disgust ...

But today, as the finger of this unknown man freely circulated through his crotch and anus, he had many emotions on his mind.

She was angry at her own helplessness.

The intruder was annoying him for the blatant advance.

She hated Paul for putting her in such a situation.

There were tears in her eyes from pain when her finger penetrated inside.

And at the same time, she was aroused when she realized that a stranger's finger was moving in her anus in a strange place.

After pushing his finger in and out of her hole for a while, he forcibly inserted a thick rubber plug into her hole.

Although the petroleum jelly reduced the discomfort somewhat, the size of the plug was much larger than the size of its hole.

But Juliet could do nothing but protest.

Juliet was trying to stop crying and take a deep breath, at that moment ...

When the plug was fully inserted inside, he smacked her sore ass hard and pulled away from her.

Juliet's literally muffled scream followed the sound of the "crack" that reverberated throughout the room.

At this point, he got very angry with Paul.

He must have told the stranger several things that are very private between the two of them.

Of course!

Besides, how could this man know that Juliet, who is always in charge at work, likes to be dominated in sex?

Although she was crying as her finger moved across her anus, she must have known that she loves to be finger poked.

And now, without worrying about the physical pain she was going through, and without anticipating what her reaction would be, she was convinced that Paul must have told her everything because of the force with which he had spanked her.

Paul had also taught her the trick of relieving extreme pain.

In the outside world, Juliet couldn't bear the loud voice of the man in front of her.

But in this private world, her biggest fantasy was that someone could torture her, force her physically.

Taking advantage of this information, he became angry and at the same time very excited when he realized that this man was playing with his body.

With all these thoughts on his mind, however, he continued to throw a whip at her.

Her pale buttocks were now reddish as cherries and hot as hell.

After ten or fifteen strokes, he threw the whip aside and began to spank Juliet's reddish buttocks.

After much torture, Juliet began to want to hug him.

He stopped and stood in front of her just when she wanted his hands to move back there for a little while longer.

Leaning down and releasing her hands, he straightened her up.

He took her delicate hand in his and lifted her up.

Juliet saw a strong rope dangling from above.

He carefully bound both of her hands and wrapped them in the rope.

He slipped and fell to the side.

The rope was tied across the bridge from the roof.

He untied the rope from its grip, took it in his hand, and began to pull it hard.

Juliet's body was being hauled up and hoisted with the rope pulling her arms.

Juliet was letting him pull on her body without any resistance.

He continued tugging on the rope until he lifted her by both heels.

Now Juliet was standing on the toes of her high heels, swinging her body, but not dangling.

He tied the end of the rope again and stood in front of her.

Juliet's entire chest was now erect as she had both arms raised.

Looking down from above, her own nipples also looked a little too angled.

And then, twirling his fingers over the dark circles around her nipples, he suddenly grabbed both pointy nipples with a pinch and tugged hard.

Screaming willingly, Juliet stumbled where she was standing.

Her thighs were also limited in her movements as her legs were tied at the bottom and her hands at the top.

He continued pulling and releasing her nipples with the pinch of his fingers.

Slowly, Juliet began to get excited again.

She wiped her eyes, drew her neck back, and moved her body toward him.

It was as if he wanted that painful pinch over and over again.

From there, he took a small amount of red cream on his fingers.

Gently, he rubbed the salve around her nipples.

He dipped his fingers into the tube again and scooped out some more cream.

Now his hand came down and began to touch her vagina.

Finding her vagina through her fine hair, he smeared the cream there as well.

Then he came back and rubbed the cream colored rubber plug on her anus.

Julieta was very excited by the touch of that cold cream on her three 'private' organs.

But after a few seconds, the cold cream started to heat her up.

And little by little it started to itch in the place where he applied the cream.

She was anxious for someone to squeeze her breasts.

She tried to free her hands to press on her own breasts, to tighten her own rigid bonds.

Right now she needed her rocky fingers, on her licked nipples and her itchy vagina ...

And at the same time he felt the touch of that vibrating object.

Paul had given her a medium vibrator, but to date she has never used it alone.

Paul used to work the vibrator on his own with her.

But now the vibrator, which had penetrated her itchy vagina, seemed too big.

Furthermore, its vibrations felt much stronger than I expected.

Although both legs were tied, she was stretching her thighs to make as much room as possible for the vibrator.

He crawled an inch, anticipating her delicate vagina.

However, Juliet was so turned on by the cream and the situation in general that she was pushing her whole body forward and trying to get the vibrator inside.

When he took the thick vibrator in its entirety, he stood shaking enjoying its vibration.

Both legs tied.

I shoot up with both hands tied.

In such an unknown place, Juliet felt the joy of life hanging completely defenseless, naked, excited in front of a stranger.

A tight plug in her anus and a vibrator filling her vagina.

Nipples turned on by that red cream on top.

She sincerely wanted the stranger to bite her, bite her, and crush her plump, fleshy buttocks.

He felt as if the two objects in both holes had penetrated deep into his body.

He had never stopped pushing the vibrator in, but Juliet herself was trying to get him in.

Closing both holes, pulling wrists and ankles to the point of tension, he stretched his entire body and with a loud cry reached the climax of happiness.

For the first time in his life, that moment lasted long.

The muscles in her anus began to tighten while her vaginal muscles began to weaken.

And before the first wave of arousal subsided, her body stiffened again.

She experienced a second orgasm in a row due to the rubber plug inserted into her anus.

She was experiencing extreme pain and pleasure at the same time.

Slowly, her body began to sink and she closed her eyes.

His face rested on his chest in a hanging position.

He leaned forward and pulled the vibrator out of her vagina.

It took a while for her body to recover.

Then, gathering a bit of strength, he raised his neck, opened his eyes and ...

... all the lights in the room were on.

Under her gaze, she saw about fifteen chairs, just ten feet from her.

She stared at the chairs in disbelief and, of course, at the people sitting in them.

There were men in their thirties and fifties ... and there were women.

They all looked at Juliet with joy and admiration.

Paul was sitting in the last chair, looking at her proudly.

I was happy to see Paul.

But then he recalled his own condition and the recent 'exposure'.

Embarrassed, she lowered her neck, but couldn't move her hands to cover her naked body.

And what was he going to hide from now?

After watching the whole 'show', they ...

With all these thoughts running through her head, she felt the brush of cold water behind her.

The stranger, who had been playing with her body for so long, was 'chilling' her with a water pipe in hand.

She had no choice but to let him bathe her with her arms and legs tied.

Turning her naked body, he bathed her completely from head to toe.

First the remains of the lashes on her buttocks, then the chafing of her arms and legs from the bandage, the breasts and nipples that swelled from the cream and its handling, in both of her delicate pores from which she suffered an unexpected attack from both directions, and all over her young and tender body.

I really needed that cold water!

When she was completely soaked, she turned off the tap and stepped forward to loosen her grip on her legs.

Julieta spread her long legs and tried to stand up straight.

Then he untied the rope that hung above and released her hands.

Leaving her alone for a moment, he approached her again.

He pulled up the back table and made Juliet sit on it.

There was no strength in his body, there was no desire in his mind to oppose any of his actions!

He laid her on the table and tied her hands.

This time he wrapped the straps around her thighs without tying her legs at the ankles.

Julieta's vagina was now more open than before, with the straps attached to hooks on either side of the table.

Now her pink vagina was visible in front of her, and the rubber plug in her rear hole was also visible.

He left her in that state for a while.

Now the thought of people sitting in the room and staring at her made her feel embarrassed and also aroused.

Remembering that Paul was also around her, she leaned back on the table, waiting for the next attack ...

And then she felt the familiar touch of the vibrator ... first on her legs, then her plump thighs, then her flat stomach, around her hollow nipples, and then slowly moving upward on both breasts, on her tight nipples.

He couldn't believe he could get excited again in such a short time.

He felt the discharge from her vagina dripping from her exhausted thighs to her own anus.

And she was overwhelmed by the sight of fifteen or twenty strangers, men and women staring at her.

Anxious, she began to pronounce:

'Ah, ah!'

Suddenly, the vibrator went off.

Juliet's arousal was no longer in her body.

She started screaming loudly, screaming and calling for the stranger to come over and continue stroking her with the vibrator.

A few seconds must have passed and then she felt a very unfamiliar and unexpected touch between her two thighs ...

Surprised, she looked there and saw that the young stranger was moving his long tongue over her vagina.

She smirked and looked at him, then leaned back on the table and relaxed her body.

He was no longer a stranger to her.

The other men and women in the room did not exist for her.

He didn't even have thoughts for Paul in his head.

Feeling the touch of the young man's long, strong tongue, he rolled his eyes and lay down.

During the next orgasm, she kept a big smile on her face.

How long she was licking her vagina, how long she was lying on the table, awake or asleep ... I had no way of knowing.

All she knew was that the two of them were alone in the room again, her limbs were free, the rubber plug had been removed from her anus and placed next to the table, and the stranger who had given her the biggest orgasm of his life, without intercourse, he stood politely in front of her.

He got up slowly and got off the table.

He had his clothes in his hands.

Now, as she dressed, he leaned against her ... not to embarrass her, but to button her tight bra.

He also kindly helped her finish dressing.

After dressing, he led Juliet back to the Watcher's hut.

The same black Mercedes was standing in front.

The Mercedes driver opened the door for her and stopped expectantly.

Julieta smiled when she remembered the friendliness of the driver.

Turning around, he asked for the first time since meeting the 'stranger',

"What's your name?"

He smiled.

He took her hand and squeezed it closer and said:

"My name is not important."

Then she just smiled and said "Thank you" and started walking towards the car.

Paul was waiting for her in the back seat of the car.

As soon as he entered, Juliet hugged Paul in her arms.

Paul patted him affectionately on the head and motioned for the driver to start the car.

The black Mercedes started running again through the narrow streets of the industrial zone toward the busy city.

Paul took a video camera that he had put aside and held its screen close to Juliet and said:

"Everything you've done since you got out of the car ... or everything that's been done to you is in this video. How brave you are."

Juliet was relaxing in his arms.

The smile on her face and the satisfaction spoke for her without needing to say anything more.

Letting her relax in the car, Paul patted her again and stared at the tape of her courage.

Today's plan was a success.

I was happy and excited that I would soon be ready for an amazing next adventure ...

END